Chapter One

TROUBLE FROM NOWHERE

Josh Ladd pulled back in surprise as a thin-faced skin diver in a black face mask burst from the sea. Josh exclaimed, "Look out!"

Seconds before, twelve-year-old Josh had been snorkeling off Molokini* islet,* thinking, *This is the life!* He had everything to make him happy—the warm Hawaiian sun, the blue-green Pacific Ocean, and Tank Catlett, his best friend, nearby. They had been feeding frozen peas and white bread to the countless, multicolored fish swarming unafraid around the boys. Then the skin diver surfaced abruptly from the clear, warm swells.

"Hey, kid," the man said as he pushed his face mask up onto his forehead. "You going back to the cat?"*

"Well," Josh began, shoving his blue face mask with snorkel onto his forehead. He remembered seeing the thin-faced man on the catamaran* during the ride from

---

*The definition and pronunciation of words marked by asterisks are contained in a glossary at the end of the book.

the island of Maui. "Yes. In a few minutes. I just ran out of bread." He held up the empty plastic wrapper.

He rode one of the six-foot swells to its peak while the man slid into the trough* of water. Josh glanced toward the sixty-foot catamaran anchored off the tiny, sunken volcano called Molokini. Only a handful of swimmers had donned masks and fins to explore the sheltered, crescent-shaped cove. Josh could see about a hundred men and women in brightly colored island clothes lining the rail to watch the swimmers.

The skin diver treaded water and glanced over his shoulder. A Windsurfer rapidly skimmed out from the islet toward them.

"Here." The man shoved a small package into Josh's hands. "Hang on to this! I'll pick it up when we're back on board. Don't let anything happen to it!"

Before Josh could protest, the man glanced at the approaching Windsurfer, pulled his mask back into place, and dived. Josh saw the diver's black fins moving rapidly, pushing the man toward the white-sand bottom. He was trailed by a school of tiny fish.

Josh heard Tank Catlett swim alongside. Tank pushed up his orange face mask and asked, "What was that all about?"

"I don't know," Josh answered with uncertainty.

He and Tank kicked their blue fins back and forth just enough to keep their heads above the swells. Both boys were wearing yellow life jackets with canisters and

The Dangerous CANOE RACE

Lee Roddy

PUBLISHING
Colorado Springs, Colorado

To my son, Steve Roddy,
whose almost total recall
of boyhood days in Hawaii
greatly enriched my own memories
of living and working there,
and who helped make this series possible

THE DANGEROUS CANOE RACE
Copyright © 1990 by Lee Roddy

Library of Congress Cataloging-in-Publication Data

Roddy, Lee, 1921–
    The dangerous canoe race.

    Summary: Twelve-year-old Josh and his friends face danger and come to a greater understanding of the importance of winning and losing when their challenger to an outrigger canoe race in the Hawaiian islands tries to win by any means.
    [1. Canoes and canoeing—Fiction. 2. Hawaii—Fiction. 3. Conduct of life—Fiction] I. Title.
PZ7.R6Dao   1990   [Fic]   90-3154
ISBN 0-929608-62-3

Published by Focus on the Family Publishing, Colorado Springs, Colorado 80903
Distributed by Word Books, Dallas, Texas.

Designer: Sherry Nicolai Russell
Cover Illustration: Ernest Norcia

Printed in the United States of America

93 94 95 / 10 9 8 7 6 5 4

CONTENTS

Acknowledgments

This novel would not be possible without the cooperation of the following people, to whom I want to express my appreciation:

Bonnie Judd of Honolulu, a true kamaaina and chairman of the Hawaii Outrigger Canoe Club. She patiently provided authentic data about this unique sport.

Weather bureau employees stationed on the different Hawaiian islands. They gave me environmental information about the weather conditions and storms used in this novel.

The Hawaii Visitors Bureau, for invaluable suggestions on people to contact and available resources for this and other upcoming stories in the series.

Although an author is solely responsible for the accuracy of details in his work, this novel would not have been possible without the assistance of those named above. To them, my heartfelt "Mahalo!"

lanyards* for instant inflation in case of emergency.

"The guy gave me this," Josh said, holding up a clear, waterproof bag with a second bag made of dark canvas inside it. "It feels like a small, metal box in here."

The boys turned to look after the diver. He was still swimming rapidly under water, trailed by a second man. Josh searched for the Windsurfer. The board floated on the surface, its sail in the water. The lone operator, called a sailor, was not in sight.

Tank ran a tanned hand through his wet, blond hair. "I heard someone on the cat' call the diver 'Rick,' but I don't know him."

"Me either," Josh answered. The boys watched as the swells lifted the Windsurfer rig on a crest. Josh glanced around, vainly trying to locate the sailor.

Between the loose Windsurfer's board and the shore, Josh glimpsed the broad, brown back of Kamuela Kong and his swimming buddy. Josh had managed to stay away from Kong all morning. Although "King" Kong was only thirteen, he had made life miserable for Josh and Tank back in Honolulu where they lived.

At that moment, Josh's attention was drawn to a swimmer struggling in rougher water. At first Josh thought it was the sailor, but then he saw that it was a boy with an orange mask and snorkel.

Josh pointed with his free hand. "Look! That kid's in trouble!"

"Sure is," Tank replied in his usual slow, easygoing

fashion. But there was a hint of excitement in his voice as he added, "I saw him on the cat'. He's got a crippled leg, remember? He didn't wear a fin on that bad leg when he went into the water."

"That's why the waves are too strong for him. Let's give him a hand before he gets cut on the coral or steps on a sea urchin!"

Josh's usual quick-moving nature took over. He shoved Rick's package into the empty plastic bread wrapper. He twisted the end of the wrapper, pulled it through a clip on his waist belt, and knotted it tightly. Then he tucked the whole bag inside the waistband of his blue and white swim trunks.

The two friends pulled down their face masks and adjusted the mouthpieces. They swam rapidly toward Molokini, which was the tip of an extinct volcano rising straight up from the ocean floor. Barely a hundred and fifty feet high, the nearly barren islet was thought by early Hawaiians to be the home of ancestral spirits. To thousands of annual visitors, it was a wonderful snorkeling area. But to the handicapped boy being swept toward the shore, Molokini was a real danger.

By the time Josh and Tank reached the area, the boy had disappeared into the troughs. Each wave rolled powerfully toward the shore.

Josh remembered seeing the boy's left leg; it was not much more than bone covered with skin. That leg was barely moving now. The single, black fin on the good right leg was not enough to keep the boy from being swept toward the islet. Like Josh and Tank, the third boy had strong upper-body and arm development. He used his arms to stay afloat, but he was helpless as a cork bouncing in the strong surf.

When Josh reached the white, tense-faced boy, he raised his face mask to his forehead. "It's okay! My friend and I'll pull you back to safety!"

The boy's hazel eyes were wide, and his sandy hair was plastered across his forehead. He nodded as Josh grabbed him under the right shoulder and Tank seized the left.

"Ready?" Josh puffed.

Both Tank and the new kid nodded. Josh shoved the mouthpiece back into place and started swimming. He felt the tip of his fins touch the sharp coral. Panic welled up within him. Josh wondered if it was too late. Desperately, fearing the awesome wounds the coral could inflict, Josh gave a swift kick and swam away from the danger.

In a few minutes, the three boys reached the high, twin, fiberglass hulls of the big catamaran. The Hawaiian captain bent down and pulled the new boy onto the steps. A moment later, with the help of the captain, Josh and Tank climbed aboard, breathing hard but feeling good.

They pulled off their face masks and fins. The mainland visitors crowded around the boys. Josh felt uncomfortable with all the attention, so he slipped away, leaving Tank and the boy in the circle of questioning people.

"Hey, what happened out there?" "That was close." "You were lucky the boys saw you."

He pulled off his life jacket and walked barefooted to where he had stored his clothes in a red nylon tote bag. He started to shove his face mask into the bag. Then he stopped, aware of the package the diver had given him.

Josh pulled the bread wrapper from where it had ridden securely between his skin and the waistband of his swim trunks. He glanced around the deck but didn't see the man who had given him the package.

Guess he'll be along soon, Josh thought as he shoved the package into his bag.

He started to walk away, but several older people in their aloha shirts* and muumuus* stopped him. They continued to exclaim over what he and Tank had done to rescue the handicapped boy.

Josh was embarrassed by the fuss. He didn't know what to say. Just then, the rescued boy limped up. He was followed by Tank, King Kong, and Kong's barrel-chested friend.

The boy said, "I'm Shawn Tremaine. I just met your friend Tank. Thanks for trying to help, but it wasn't necessary. I could have handled things out there by myself."

Josh blinked in surprise.

Tank whispered under his breath, "Well, pardon us for saving your life!"

Kong leaned forward with his face close to the new boy. Kong spoke pidgin English which all the local kids of

many national origins understood. "Hey, you, malihini!*
Why foh you do da kine dumb stunt like dat, huh? You
got no leg! You drown easy!"

Josh was startled by Shawn's sharp answer. "I can do
anything you can do!"

Kong growled, "You pupule,* Bruddah!* Nobody beat
Kong!"

"What's *pupule* mean?" Shawn turned and asked Josh.

"Means 'crazy' in Hawaiian," Josh answered. He
touched the newcomer's pale white arm lightly and said
in a whisper, "Listen, Shawn. That's Kong! Don't mess
with him!"

Shawn pulled away and looked straight at Kong.

"Crazy, am I? You want to race or something?"

Kong glanced at Shawn's crippled leg and sneered.
"Dumb malihini can't race!"

Shawn snapped, "Oh, yeah? Try me!"

Josh let out a groan, "No, Shawn!"

Kong asked, "How 'bout da kine canoe race?"

"Canoe?" the newcomer repeated, glancing at Josh,
who shook his head in warning. Shawn didn't seem to
notice. "I've raced canoes lots of times on lakes and
rivers, but I didn't think you could use them on the
ocean."

Kong sneered at the new boy's ignorance. "Not da kine
canoe for malihinis; Hawaiian canoe!"

"Hawaiian canoe?" Shawn asked.

Josh whispered, "He means an outrigger canoe. It's

got a couple arms, which are attached to a pontoon* that floats in the water and keeps the canoe from tipping over so easily."

Shawn exclaimed, "Oh, yes! I've seen pictures of them, but I've never been in one." He turned to Kong again. "You want to race me in one of those?"

Kong made a big sweeping motion with his strong right arm. "Race from where we start dis mornin' 'round dis place from Maui to Molokini. Da losers is slaves to da winnahs foh one week! Okay, malihini?"

"Don't do it, Shawn." Josh cried, gripping the handicapped boy's arm.

"You're on!" Shawn cried.

Josh and Tank groaned in unison.

"When?" Kong demanded, smiling broadly, sure of victory.

"Soon as I get a canoe," Shawn replied. "And a paddle or whatever I'll need."

Kong's thick lips curled into a sneer. "Outrigger canoe not da kine for one person! Need planty* paddlers! Six!"

"Six?" Shawn answered thoughtfully. "Well, I don't know anybody in Hawaii except this guy I met at the hotel."

He pointed to a boy of about twelve standing next to Tank.

"Not me! No way!" The boy shook his head vigorously.

Shawn's face fell. "Well, I suppose I can find some

other guys to help me paddle."

"You got two already!" Kong said and thrust a thick, brown forefinger in Josh's glistening-wet chest. "An' da kine Tank!" Kong added, jabbing the same finger into the blond-headed boy's shoulder.

Josh started to protest, but Tank beat him to it. "No fair! Kong, you've been paddling canoes all your life! None of us has ever even been in one."

"No mattah, Bruddah!" Kong said triumphantly, smiling "Kong say you all paddle canoe in race, or Kong make all of you wish you dead!"

Josh started to protest again but glanced at Shawn's pleading eyes and changed his mind. Josh turned to Tank. "How'd we get ourselves in this mess?"

Tank muttered under his breath, "Maybe we should have left him out there alone in the water."

"You guys, don't worry!" Shawn exclaimed, limping closer. "We'll show them who's the best! And we'll win, too!"

"Oh, sure!" Tank grumbled. "We'll all win a week of being slave to a guy who would make Simon Legree* look like a kindly old grandfather!"

Josh didn't say anything. He looked at the kid with the handicapped leg and then at the bully. Kong was swaggering about the deck, bragging and waving his massive arms. Josh got a sick taste in his mouth, remembering how many times Kong had picked on him and Tank.

Josh felt a sudden, powerful urge to get even. He

exclaimed, "Tank, let's beat Kong!"

"Wh-what?" Tank stammered. "Beat Kong in an outrigger canoe race?"

Shawn nodded enthusiastically. "Why not?"

"There's every reason in the world why we can't and not one reason why we can!" Tank grumbled.

Josh reached out and gripped his friend's forearm. "Kong's made us look bad ever since we moved here. Now here's our chance to get even!"

The minute he said it, Josh felt a little guilty. Getting even wasn't something he was supposed to do. But in that moment, that's exactly what he wanted.

When the big catamaran docked at Maalaea Bay,* Josh picked up his duffel bag and went ashore. He had forgotten about the mysterious package he carried. He had no idea it was taking him straight into danger. He was too busy thinking about the canoe race.

Chapter Two

A MYSTERIOUS PHONE CALL

Back in Honolulu, Josh walked up the outside stairs of his apartment building, swinging his nylon tote bag. He wore zoris,* cutoffs and an old aloha shirt.* His thoughts were filled with how they were going to prepare for the canoe race. The doubt he felt offset his desire to beat King Kong.

"What have I got myself into?" Josh wondered aloud.

"Josh," Tank called from the ground floor of the concrete-block apartment where he lived. Josh stopped climbing the stairs and looked over the rail down at Tank.

"We'll beat him!" his blond-haired friend yelled through cupped hands.

"Sure will!" Josh answered.

Josh heard the screen door shut as Tank went inside the apartment that he shared with his parents and older sister. Josh turned to finish climbing the stairs just as another friend's face appeared above Josh at the lanai* railing on the third floor.

"What are you two malihinis* going to win?" Roger

11

Okamoto asked, looking down at Josh. Typical of the local islanders, his voice went up at the end of each sentence. Roger was thirteen, slender, with copper-tan skin and black hair that stuck out above his ears.

Josh tipped his head back sharply to look up. "A canoe race from Maui to Molokini* and back."

"Oh, yeah?" Roger's dark brown eyes opened wide with interest. "Who're you going to race?"

"King Kong."

Roger's mouth dropped open. "You've been out in the sun too long, Josh!"

"It wasn't my idea!" Josh protested, feeling uneasy. "Tank and I met this new kid on the catamaran,* and he challenged Kong. Then Kong insisted Tank and I be on this new kid's team."

Josh decided not to mention his own desire to get even with Kong.

Roger sadly shook his head. "Are you really serious about beating Kong?"

"Sure! Why not?" Josh tried to sound confident.

"I can tell you why not! You got pilikia!* Kong was practically born in a canoe. You and Tank have never even seen one up close, have you?"

"Well, no, but—"

"You'd be better off trying to outswim a great white shark!"

Josh swallowed hard and answered with a confidence he didn't feel. "We can beat him!"

Roger groaned and rolled his eyes helplessly toward the clear blue Hawaiian sky. "Do you have any idea of what's involved in an outrigger canoe race, Josh?"

"Do you?" Josh challenged.

"Shuh t'ing, Bruddah!"* Roger answered, slipping into pidgin as locals often did. "I belong to da kine* canoe club 'til last year."

Josh's hopes soared. "Hey! You can be on our team! Teach us how—"

"You pupule,* Bruddah!" Roger interrupted. "You on your own!"

"Well then, will you at least teach Tank and me and this new guy, Shawn, about canoe racing?"

Roger considered, frowning thoughtfully as he gazed down from the upper lanai railing. "Okay," he said, "but don't think you guys are going to talk me into racing Kong!"

"Mahalo!"* Josh exclaimed. "How about tomorrow morning?"

"Fine! I'll meet you at the boat house on the Ala Wai Canal."*

Josh climbed the last few steps to his apartment and removed his zoris before entering. It was an Oriental custom that many haoles* adopted when they moved to the fiftieth state.

Through the sliding screen door, he heard a sound and called out, "Mom?"

Josh's fourteen-year-old sister, Tiffany, replied from

inside the apartment. "She's shopping with Tank's mother." As he slid the screen door open and stepped barefoot inside the cool living room, Tiffany asked, "What did I hear you telling Roger about a canoe race?"

Josh was sorry his sister had overheard him. Tiffany sometimes seemed to take a superior attitude toward him, as if he wasn't old enough to come in out of the rain, even though he was just two years younger than she.

He walked across the off-white rug, carrying his bag. Trade winds, which some people called "nature's air conditioning," blew softly through the open louvered windows. The warm breezes lightly ruffled his sister's short, brunette hair. She was sprawled on a rattan chair with tropical print cushions. She wore white shorts with a blue and white tank top. A book lay open on her bare, brown legs.

"Where is everybody?" Josh asked, hoping to change the subject. He set the nylon bag down on the arm of the matching sofa.

"They're all down at Waikiki Beach.* Dad and Nathan are taking a quick dip in the ocean before dinner. Grandma went along to watch."

Nathan was ten years old and the youngest member of the Ladd family. Grandma Ladd, who was widowed, had just joined them a couple of weeks before.

Josh picked up his bag. He wondered how his father would react to news of the canoe race. "I'm going to read." He padded barefoot across the carpet and started down the hallway toward the room he shared with Nathan.

Tiffany called, "You didn't answer my question."

"Tell you later."

The moment he said it, Josh realized it was the wrong thing to have done. He knew Tiffany would be suspicious.

"Come back here!" she called, her voice taking on the big-sister tone she often used. "Tell me what kind of trouble you're getting into!"

Josh tossed his bag onto the upper bunk bed and raised his voice. "It's nothing. Just forget it!"

He heard Tiffany coming down the hallway. "You're up to something," she cried accusingly. "And it's probably dangerous, too."

"Aw, Tif," Josh replied with an injured tone, sticking his head out the bedroom doorway. "Why're you so suspicious?"

"Because I know you!" Tiffany stood at the end of the hallway, hands on hips. "Now, are you going to tell me, or will Dad have to ask you?"

Josh fought down anger at his sister's implied threat to tell on him. "Oh, all right!" he growled, going back down the hallway to face her.

He started to tell her about Shawn, then paused, frowning. "Hey! I forgot something! Be right back." He ran back to his room and unzipped his bag. He pulled out his fins and mask.

For a moment, Josh stared at the package the skin diver had asked him to hold. *Wonder why he didn't pick it up on the trip back to Maalaea Bay?** Josh thought. He pulled it out of the bread wrapper and felt the sealed package, containing a canvas bag. It seemed to have a metal box inside. He had no idea what it contained. And he didn't know how to find the man who had given it to him.

Tiffany called, "What's going on?"

"Just checking my stuff," Josh answered in a loud voice. "Be right there."

He decided not to say anything about the mysterious package, so he stuffed it back into the tote bag.

He told his sister how he and Tank had rescued Shawn. Josh explained about Kong's challenge, and how all three boys were going to race Kong when they found three more paddlers.

"Hmm," Tiffany mused, placing her long, slender fingers on her chin. "An outrigger canoe race might be just the way to put that big bully in his place!"

Her response surprised Josh. He had expected Tiffany to give him one of her sisterly lectures on what a dumb thing he had done.

Josh asked cautiously, "Do you really think so?"

"Well, it's a cinch you and Tank won't get any peace from Kong the way things are going. But if you could beat him at something where he's practically an expert. . . .Hey! You know what would be really neat?"

"What?"

"If you had some girls in your canoe!"

"Girls?" Josh's surprise almost made him strangle on the word.

"Why not?" Tiffany demanded, turning to face him. Her eyes shone with excitement. "You need three more paddlers! Marsha and I could—"

"Hold it," Josh interrupted. Marsha was Tank's older sister, also age fourteen. "Canoeing requires lots of muscles. It's a sport for boys and men!"

Tiffany whirled on him, blue eyes blazing. "I remember reading a magazine article about a whole bunch of champion athletes from all kinds of sports. You know what the article decided? Huh? Do you?"

"No, what?" he asked without enthusiasm.

"I remember exactly what the article said: 'Winning is in the mind and not the muscles!' "

Josh sighed in resignation. "You and Shawn should get along great, Tif! You both seem to think alike!"

"I'd like to meet him. When are you seeing him again?"

"He's going to call tonight."

"Good! Then it's settled." Tiffany turned triumphantly and ran across the rug toward the door.

"No, it's not settled," Josh cried. "And where are you going?"

"To tell Marsha." Tiffany slid open the screen door and bent down to pull on her zoris. Then she fairly flew down the concrete stairs toward the Catletts' ground floor apartment.

"Oh, no!" Josh moaned, slapping the flat of his hand

on the cool, concrete block wall. "I can't believe this is happening! First this guy, Rick, forgets to pick up his package. Then I get talked into racing Kong, and now the girls want to be in the race!"

Slowly, Josh turned and walked to the sliding screen door that opened onto the lanai. He stood staring moodily toward Diamond Head.* The ancient volcanic landmark rose brown and ugly in the late summer sky. It was a peaceful scene, yet Josh felt a growing uneasiness inside. A mynah bird* called from the shade of a be-still tree* covered with bright yellow blossoms.

Wait until Dad hears about this, Josh thought, trying to cheer himself up. *He won't let Tiffany race in a canoe! And Grandma and Mom will agree, too.*

Feeling a little better, Josh picked up his swim trunks and draped them over the lanai rail to dry. Then he hurried to his room and took the package out of the tote bag.

"Rick," Josh mused aloud. "Tank said he had heard someone call him that. But how will he find me? Or how will I find him? Guess I'll just have to wait and see."

Josh placed the mysterious package on the top shelf in his closet. He closed the door and sat down at a small desk by the louvered window. He flipped through the few books on Hawaii he had picked up since moving to the islands.

Nothing! Not one word about outrigger canoe races, he thought with disappointment. His blue eyes skimmed the books again. Animals, birds, diving, surfing, history—everything except canoes! Disgusted, he flopped on his bed.

Suddenly he remembered where he might get some information on canoe racing. Scrambling off his bed, he ran down the hallway into the living room. He snatched up the telephone directory and flipped rapidly through it. "Yeah! This should do it."

He picked up the phone and dialed carefully. "Hello? Is this the Canoe Club? I'd like to talk with someone who can tell me about racing outriggers."

"I'll transfer you," a male voice said. A moment later a woman came on the line.

"Hi! My name's Josh Ladd," he said. "I'm interested in knowing about racing outrigger canoes. Can you help me?"

"I'll try," the woman replied. "I'm Arlene Simons. What do you want to know?"

Josh hesitated, "Well, uh...I don't even know where to begin. But...well, are six people really needed to paddle an outrigger?"

"There are various size canoes." She had a patient, pleasant voice. "The most common is the six-man type."

"Six men?"

"Or women," Arlene Simons chuckled. "Women race, too, you know."

Josh stifled a groan, thinking of what would happen if Tiffany and Marsha convinced their parents they should be allowed to be in the race.

"I see," Josh said, picking up a pencil by the phone. "Tell me about a six-person canoe, please."

"Well, there are two main types of outriggers. One's made of koa* wood. It's very hard and expensive. Most people use fiberglass canoes now. They're less expensive and not as heavy."

Josh poised his pencil over the note pad. "How heavy are they?"

"They weigh four hundred pounds."

Josh almost dropped the pencil. "Four?. . ."

The woman added, "Outriggers are about forty feet long."

Josh groaned softly into the phone.

"Did you say something?" the voice in his ear asked with concern.

Josh answered, "No, not really."

His mind was leaping with questions. *Where will we ever get enough money for an outrigger canoe?*

"You'll probably want to know where each of the paddlers sits in the canoe and how the paddling is done," Arlene Simons continued. "Are you writing this down, Josh?"

"I'm writing."

"There are five paddlers," the woman's voice continued, "plus a steersman who strokes whenever he can. The first paddler is in the very front or bow* of the canoe. He's called One Seat. The person behind him is called Two Seat, and he calls commands."

Josh's fingers were cramped when he finally stopped scribbling down all the information Arlene gave him. He thanked her and hung up the phone with a long, deep sigh.

What have I got myself into? Josh wondered. He had a sinking feeling in the pit of his stomach. *Everything is against us!*

The ringing telephone broke into his thoughts. The sound was different from that made by mainland phones. This one was more like a bird chirping. Josh picked it up. "Hello. Ladd family residence."

A man's voice asked, "You the kid who's holding a package given to you out at Molokini this morning?"

"Oh, yes! Hi!" Josh exclaimed. "I looked for you on the catamaran."

"Can't talk now! Call you later!" The phone clicked and went dead.

Josh stared moodily at the receiver. "Now what did that mean?" he asked himself.

He heard his father's car pull into the carport behind the apartment. He decided not to say anything about the package or the brief phone call he had just had. But the whole thing was beginning to make him nervous, even though he wasn't sure why.

Chapter Three

THE FAMILY RALLIES AROUND

Josh slipped on his zoris* and slap-slapped down the stairs; he had to tell his dad about Kong's canoe race challenge. Josh's father, John Ladd, helped Grandma out of the white station wagon. The fenders were rusted from the salty ocean air. Nathan, Josh's younger brother, slid out of the open window at the tailgate. His hair was still wet from swimming.

"How was your trip to Molokini?"* Nathan asked. He swung his green nylon swim trunks at the end of his right forefinger "See any sharks or moray eels?"

"No," Josh answered, "it was too rough for good snorkeling, so we had to come back early." He walked over to his grandmother.

She finished stuffing her ever-present knitting into a bag. One knitting needle was stuck into her gray hair. She always greeted Josh with a kiss on the cheek, although he was at the age he didn't even want his own mother to kiss him—especially in public. He reached up, pulled the needle from his grandmother's hair and handed it to her.

"Hi, Grandma," he said, as she bent down to kiss his cheek. "How did you like Waikiki Beach?"*

"It was beautiful, Joshua," she replied with a smile. Grandma Ladd was tall and slender, much like her son who was six feet tall. She wore her hair in soft waves that ended just above the neck of her gaily colored Hawaiian print muumuu.* "Did I hear you say you went on that trip and couldn't even go in the water?"

"Only a few of us went snorkeling, Grandma," Josh answered.

He squirmed uneasily, his mind tumbling with ways to tell his father about what had really happened at Molokini. He tried an indirect approach. "Dad, did you ever see a Hawaiian outrigger canoe?"

"Yes, one time I saw some Hawaiians paddling out of Kewalo Basin* in an outrigger. It was beautiful to see the way they paddled the canoe together."

Josh sensed that his father, a former California school teacher now publishing a Honolulu tourist paper, was going to tell Josh more than he really wanted to know.

Mr. Ladd followed Grandma onto the stairs and said over his shoulder, "The native paddlers seemed to move as one person. Every stroke was in perfect harmony. I've never seen such precision outside of a machine. Why do you ask?"

Josh took a deep breath and briefly explained about Shawn's rescue and Kong's challenge to a canoe race.

The family had reached the apartment, removed their shoes, and entered the living room before Josh had finished telling about the Molokini experience.

Nathan was the first to react. He turned shining eyes up at his big brother. "Wow! You're dumb enough to try beating Kong in a canoe race?"

"Nathan," their father said firmly, "that's no way to talk to your brother!"

Josh plopped heavily into a rattan chair. "Dad, I had no choice about the race. What could I do?"

"I don't know, Josh." His father answered as he walked into the kitchen. "I don't like the sound of this. You should have waited until we talked it over. Are you sure that the only reason you agreed to be in the race was because Kong insisted on it?"

Josh hesitated, unwilling to admit he wanted to get even with Kong.

Nathan saved Josh from having to answer. "Dad, would you please bring me a root beer?"

Mr. Ladd called back, "In a minute. Anybody else want anything?" Josh heard the refrigerator door open.

Grandma Ladd sat down in an easy chair and removed her knitting from the bag. "I don't believe I care for anything, thank you, John." She looked at her oldest grandson. "Joshua, now that you're into this difficult situation, what are your plans?"

"I haven't made any, Grandma, but I'm working on it." For a moment, Josh secretly hoped his father might forbid him to participate in the race. But he had given his word to Shawn. If Josh backed out now, it would make terrible problems for Shawn and cause even worse problems with Kong.

Kong would probably think Josh had used his father to get out of the race. Kong would then go out of his way to make life even more difficult for Josh, especially when school started. But if they beat Kong, he would have to consider Josh, Tank and Shawn in a better light. It would feel great to beat Kong, too.

Josh glanced toward the kitchen door as his father returned with two cold cans of soda. "Then you don't mind, Dad?"

"Yes, I do mind, Son." John Ladd handed a frosty can of root beer to Nathan and sat down on the sofa beside Grandma. "But perhaps you need to learn something from this experience."

"Like what?" Nathan asked before Josh could speak.

"Like letting people put you into a situation in which you don't want to really be involved. And what the consequences will be."

Josh looked sharply at his father. "You mean, you think we're going to lose the race?"

"I didn't say that, Son! You made a commitment without thinking, so—to answer your question—I think you're honor-bound to fulfill that commitment."

"Well said, John!" Josh's grandmother exclaimed with a clap of her hands. Turning to Josh she said, "You can do it!"

Josh watched his grandmother adjust her pale, flesh-colored, plastic glasses on her nose. Then her fingers returned to the knitting. Josh asked, "Do you really think I can win, Grandma?"

She nodded emphatically. "If you have the desire."

"Oh, I have that!" Josh answered with feeling.

Grandma continued, "And if you also have the discipline and an effective plan, you certainly could win the race." She reached over and touched the boy's hand. "I'll help you, too!"

Nathan asked in surprise. "How can you help, Grandma?"

Grandma Ladd smiled confidently. "I'll begin by researching the subject. Joshua, you inquire around the neighborhood for anyone who has had canoeing experience."

"Roger has." Josh pointed upward, indicating the apartment above. "But he won't paddle. I already asked him."

"Don't be too sure about that," Grandma said with a faint smile. "John, would you mind asking your friend Sam Catlett if he has any contacts in his business who might be helpful to us in this venture?"

"He's a department store manager. What would he know about outrigger canoe racing?"

"I don't know, John. That's why I'd appreciate it if you asked him." Grandma's fingers fairly flew, making the knitting needles clack, as her excitement grew. She turned to Nathan. "You could help by asking your little friends if they have older brothers who might wish to be part of the victory team."

"Victory team?" Nathan echoed, his tone showing disbelief. "You really think Josh can beat King Kong?"

"I have faith," Grandma said. "I didn't come to the Hawaiian Islands to see my oldest grandson humiliated by some bully!"

Josh wanted to jump up and cheer, but a tinge of guilt swept over him. Grandma would not approve of his desire for revenge.

Josh said quietly, "Thanks, Grandma."

"Then we're all agreed?" Grandma spoke in a crisp, quick tone of voice, indicating the source of her son's and grandson's fast-moving, quick-thinking personalities. "John? How about it?"

When he nodded, Grandma asked, "Nathan?"

"Aw, Grandma, Josh can't beat King Kong!"

The older woman said firmly, "Nathan, anybody can find the negatives in life."

Nathan hesitated, then said, "Well, okay, I guess. But what about Mom and Tiffany?"

Josh reluctantly confessed, "Tif wants to be a paddler. She's trying to talk Marsha into helping, too."

"Great!" Grandma cried, waving a knitting needle in midair. "That leaves only your mother to persuade! I'll talk to her."

"Well, Son," John Ladd said, "now that we've agreed

to help with the race, we'll have to set our goals and decide how to achieve them."

Grandma absentmindedly stuck one needle in her hair and began pushing her knitting back into the bag. "Perhaps we can discuss that when everyone's here for dinner. Meanwhile, you heard your father. Let's all get busy!"

Josh jumped up from his chair. "I'll go ask my friend Manuel. I'll bet he knows about canoe racing."

A few minutes later, Josh had dashed down the street, scattering a flock of mynah birds.* They always seemed to be in the driveway or on the sidewalk. Josh slowed as he approached a small board-and-batten house. It was typical of older Hawaiian homes, resting high off the ground to discourage subterranean termites that would eat the wooden dwelling from the inside. The little soft-bodied, almost transparent-looking insects were a major problem in Hawaii's wooden structures.

"Hey, Manuel!" Josh called as he pushed the sagging wire gate open and ran up the short path in the front yard. Josh was only vaguely aware of the banana trees* rustling in the gentle trade winds and the sweet fragrance of the plumeria* blossoms. "Manuel, you home?"

He didn't answer, so Josh leaped up on the high front porch and knocked hard. A moment later, he heard the sound of bare feet coming from inside the house. He tried to appear casual by leaning against the wooden post that supported the porch's tin roof. *Don't be too eager,* Josh cautioned himself.

Manuel, with dark, wavy hair and deep brown eyes, was a top student in school. He was considered by the other neighborhood kids to be very akamai.* He pushed the screen door open with his bare foot.

"You pau* snorkeling at Molokini already?"

Josh nodded, then asked, "You got a minute?"

Manuel opened the door wider. "Come in." He was dressed like Josh in cutoffs and zoris* but didn't have on a shirt.

Josh asked, "Your mom home?"

"She's doing the laundry. We can go back to my room to talk."

Josh followed Manuel down the hallway. The boy's bedroom was small but well-lighted from open louvered windows. Josh's eyes barely skimmed the familiar surfing posters on the wall and a crucifix hanging from a nail over the stacked double bunk beds. Josh's eyes quickly found what he had remembered from previous visits.

"You sure have a lot of boat models, Manuel." Josh pointed to the shelf above a small desk. "Where did you get this one of an outrigger canoe?"

Manuel wasn't considered akamai without reason. He didn't answer but turned thoughtful brown eyes on his visitor. "Why are you suddenly interested in outriggers, Josh?"

"I'm going to be in a race with one."

"Yeah? Against whom?"

Josh squirmed a little, but he evaded the question so

he could pose one of his own. "Did you ever race one?"

"Lots of times. Why? Are you looking for paddlers?"

"Would you like to be one?"

"Why don't you answer my question first. Against whom?"

Josh took a short breath and said softly, "Kamuela Kong."

"King Kong?" Manuel laughed, showing even, white teeth. "Why in the world would anyone in his right mind race that guy?"

"Maybe because there's no choice."

Manuel turned serious eyes on his visitor. "You sure there was no choice?"

Josh thought of his secret desire to get even with Kong and shrugged. "I need experienced paddlers. Will you be one?"

"What's the reward for beating him?"

"Wouldn't it be enough just to win over Kong?"

"I guess so, but more important, what's the penalty for losing?"

"The losers serve the winners for one week."

Manuel mused, "In other words, your whole future depends on winning this race?"

Josh swallowed hard but nodded. "I hadn't thought of it quite that way, but I guess so. At least, my future happiness. If we don't win the race, Kong will make life miserable for Tank and me when school starts. But if we win, Kong will leave us alone. Maybe he'll even treat us a little more like equals."

"But if you lose. . .hmm." Manuel picked up the model outrigger and studied it, leaving his thought unfinished. Then he continued, "I've watched Kong paddling on the Ala Wai Canal, and I'm sure he has a weakness."

"He has? What?"

"You still got your video camera?"

"Yes, why?"

"You can use it to beat Kong."

Josh blinked in surprise and gave Manuel a puzzled look.

Manuel replaced the model and turned around. "Will you use the video camera the way I show you so that Kong can be beaten in this race?"

"Sure!" Josh almost exploded with excitement. "Anything you say!"

Manuel nodded. "Then I'll help."

"You will?"

"Absolutely! Now, sit down. Let's see what you've got so far and what you'll need to do to win."

Josh's hopes spiraled happily upward as he dropped to the rug made of grass squares. He listened eagerly to Manuel's words as he summarized the situation.

"We need five paddlers and a steersman to race. You've only got four paddlers: you, Tank, this new kid, Shawn, and me. If Tiffany and Marsha—"

"We need boys," Josh interrupted. "Strong boys, like big kanakas,* if we can find them! Not girls!"

"Muscles are important, of course," Manuel continued thoughtfully, "but so's thinking!" He tapped his forehead with the fingers of his right hand. "Since we don't have the physical strength of Kong and his friends, we'll have to be more akamai. Let me think on this tonight, and then meet me tomorrow morning at the boat house. Okay?"

"Okay." Josh stood. "You think we can really win?"

"We can, if we do everything just right. But it could be dangerous."

Chapter Four

A SURPRISE AT THE CANAL

Josh's spirits were high as he rushed back toward the two rows of three-story apartment buildings where he lived. They stood only a few feet apart. Josh's family lived in the second row of apartments. Diamond Head loomed to the left. The ancient brown volcano slanted gradually upward for a short distance. Then its sides seemed to go straight up like castle walls.

Just as Josh entered the apartment, the phone rang. No one else was home, so Josh answered the phone.

"Hello," he said, wondering if it was the skin diver wanting his package.

"Josh? This is Shawn. Great news! My folks rented a canoe for us! We can see it tomorrow morning about nine o'clock at the boat house on the Ala Wai Canal.* Do you know where that is?"

"Yes. I'm going to meet a kid named Manuel there. Say, did you have any luck finding paddlers?"

"I told you; I don't know anybody here. I'm going to have to leave that up to you and Tank. Well, see you

33

tomorrow."

Josh replaced the phone with some annoyance, think-ing, *Shawn's big mouth got us into this mess, and now he wants us to find all the paddlers. I better go find Tank.*

Josh ran back down the stairs to Tank's apartment. As he started across the driveway, he heard someone call his name. It was King Kong, standing by the be-still tree.*

"Hey, haole* boy!" Kong called. "You ready to race?"

Josh felt uneasy talking to Kong. Although he was just thirteen, he was almost six feet tall and weighed around two hundred pounds. Josh replied carefully, "We think we've got a canoe lined up, but we're still trying to find enough paddlers."

Kong grinned, his mouth spreading without humor. "You got one month!"

"One month?"

"Thi'ty days!" Kong said emphatically. He started to turn back toward the twenty-foot-high wall of bamboo and oleanders.*

"That's impossible!"

Kong ignored the remark. He changed the subject. "Hey, Bruddah,* you in some kind pilikia?"*

Josh shook his head. "No, I'm not in any trouble. Why?"

"Dis guy Rick look for you. I know him long time. He call me, ask foh phone so he can call you. He planty* huhu."*

An uneasiness crept over Josh as he thought about the

package hidden in his closet. "Why should he be angry with me?" he asked Kong.

"He say you got something belong him, but dah 'nother guy, he want it, too."

Josh felt his stomach twist a little. "What other guy?"

Kong shrugged and started walking way. "Ask Rick," he said over his massive shoulder. Then Kong stopped and half-smiled. "Maybe so you be bettah off give Kong da kine* t'ing Rick want. Maybe so he pay me, but you off dah hook from him and dah other kine guy."

"I can't do that." Josh shook his head.

"Thi'ty days, den!" Kong eased though a hole in the oleanders and bamboo. "No time have pilikia with da kine Rick or dah other guy!"

Josh hurried to find Tank and repeated what Kong had said.

Tank replied, "Josh, I don't like this at all! Who's this other guy Kong's talking about? Wonder why he wants that package?"

Josh took a slow breath and let it out. "I wish I knew! But all I can do is wait until Rick calls again."

"Hmm,...it sounds strange. I wonder what's in that package?"

Josh said, "I don't have the foggiest idea. But it's bothering me. There's something spooky about that whole thing."

Tank suggested, "Maybe we should take a look in that package."

"I can't do that!"

"Sure, you could!" Tank's usual slow speech was speeding up with excitement. "Don't you see that there's something strange about this? First of all, why did he give it to you like he did in the water and then swim away? Then how did he find you? And why wouldn't he tell you where to return the package to him?"

Josh shook his head and walked across the parking lot toward the apartment building. A sense of fear gave him a creepy feeling. "I don't know. I would like to give the package to Rick and forget about it."

Josh waited all afternoon to hear from Rick, but he didn't call. He wondered what was in the package, but he would not open it because it wasn't his. That evening, his entire family helped him make plans for the canoe race.

Grandma had even done research at the library and reported that they would need a Boston Whaler, which was an open speedboat. The powerboat would carry relief paddlers and follow the canoe during the race in case a bad storm arose or if they ran into any trouble.

The next morning, when Josh awoke his stomach felt tight. He wondered how they would find enough boys to join their canoe racing team. They especially needed two big strong paddlers for the fourth and fifth seats. The young men who sat in these positions were called the 'engine.' And where would they get a speedboat?

Josh threw back the sheet and slid off the top bunk.

He landed quietly on his bare feet, trying to avoid awakening his little brother, who slept in the bottom bunk. Josh went to the closet and opened the door. He reached up on the shelf for the package the diver had given him.

Nathan called sleepily, "What're you doing?"

Josh jerked back his hand and said, "Nothing. Go back to sleep."

"What happens when you're racing Kong and there's a big bad storm and your canoe sinks?"

"It won't. Besides, that's why the Boston Whaler will run along with us." Josh went into the bathroom and closed the door.

"Where are you going to get that boat?" Nathan called through the door. "Can I drive it? What if it rains real hard and you can't see the Boston Whaler? Or what if we can't see you and then you sink in the ocean?"

Josh didn't answer, but he growled to himself as he reached for his toothbrush. "Little brothers can be such a pain!" As Josh brushed his teeth, he thought, *I wish Rick would call so I can get rid of that package! I wonder what Kong meant about another guy wanting it?*

Nathan continued to pester Josh with questions through the closed bathroom door, but he ignored his brother. He hurried to dress so he could have breakfast before he met with Tank.

After breakfast, Josh obtained his mother's permission to meet Shawn at the Ala Wai Canal. He picked up the video camera from the closet and joined Tank in the parking lot. It was late July, one of the warmest months of the year. The temperature would reach nearly 90 degrees later in the day. The humidity was above 60 percent, so it felt damp and muggy.

Tank said, "This whole race thing is getting me down. Last night I saw news on the TV about an outrigger canoe that got caught in a squall and sank."

"My little brother was bugging me this morning about what would happen if we got caught by a storm."

Tank continued, "These guys got separated from their Boston Whaler because nobody could see anything until the squall passed. They were rescued, but they were stuck out in the ocean a long time. You know, that could happen to us. Good thing my parents didn't see that newscast, or they wouldn't let me race."

Josh forced a grin. "You're sure cheerful!"

Tank shrugged. "Guess this race has me more worried than I want to admit. And I don't like what Kong said yesterday about that package and the diver who gave it to you. Did he call again?"

"No, not yet. But I've been thinking about that. You remember how he popped up right in front of me in the ocean?"

"Yes," said Tank, with a questioning look on his face.

"Do you remember seeing the sailor on a Windsurfer come shooting out from Molokini* about that time?"

"Yeah! But a minute later his board was bouncing around by itself on the waves."

Josh said, "I'm wondering if Rick saw the Windsurfer and was afraid he was after him. Rick gave me the package and then disappeared under water. A minute later, the sailor was gone from the board, and there was a swimmer diving after Rick. Could it have been the sailor?"

"Could have been!" Tank said with excitement. "But why didn't the sailor go after you instead of Rick?"

"Maybe the sailor didn't see Rick give me the package."

"Hmm. Yeah, that's possible."

"We know Rick escaped because he phoned me," Josh added. "Maybe the reason he couldn't talk was because the second guy was watching him or something."

"Yeah, but if that sailor was after Rick and he finds out you've got the package, then he'll come after you. So you'd better get rid of it when we get back!"

"I can't do a thing until Rick calls."

Tank said, "You could give the package to Kong."

Josh shook his head. "That wouldn't be right." Then his face brightened. "Maybe Rick'll call by the time I get home again, and I'll just turn the package over to him. Then we can concentrate on winning the race."

"Let's hope so," Tank said with doubt.

The friends turned left on Ala Wai Boulevard, which ran parallel to the Ala Wai Canal. The canal stretched from behind Waikiki* toward downtown Honolulu, eventually curved away from the Koolau Range* and emptied into the Pacific Ocean. Several people were rowing small boats in the calm water.

The sun was still shining, but a sudden, brief shower fell on the boys from a passing cloud. It was so hot that it was refreshing, and they knew their shorts and T-shirts would dry quickly.

Josh pointed. "There's Shawn."

Shawn limped rapidly toward the boys. "Hi!" he called. "You'll like the canoe my folks rented for us!"

Suddenly, Josh pointed down the canal toward an outrigger that was just coming into sight. "Look, you guys. There's Kong. He's already practicing!"

"Sure is!" Shawn replied. "Kong and his five paddlers have been showing off for me. Watch! They're really fast."

"Just what we needed to hear," Tank moaned.

The three boys watched as the outrigger skimmed toward them on the canal's calm waters. Two slightly-curved arms extended from the left side of the canoe to a single pontoon. It rested on the water to give the craft stability and kept it from tipping easily.

Kong was in the front position. He drove his paddle into the water, bending his powerful shoulders with every thrust. His crew lifted their paddles in unison. The wet blades glistening in the sunlight dipped into the water in one rhythmic motion. The canoe shot forward smoothly and easily.

Josh let out a low whistle. "They really are fast!" He raised the video camera to his right shoulder and looked into the viewfinder. He pushed the *On* button. Josh heard a quiet hum as the tape began recording Kong and his crew of racers. The rounded black microphone mounted above the lens was recording every sound.

"Wow!" Tank muttered in awe. "Look at them go!"

"They're good," Josh agreed. "Seems like all the local boys were born with a paddle in their hands."

A car pulled up and stopped behind Josh, Tank and Shawn. Josh punched the *Off* button and turned around to see who was in the car.

Manuel jumped out and closed the door behind him. He waved. "Thanks, Mom!" The car pulled away.

He walked swiftly toward the boys. "Hi, Josh. Tank. I thought I'd find you here. You must be Shawn."

Shawn nodded and said, "Hi."

Josh said, "Shawn, this is Manuel. Manuel, we're watching Kong practice."

All four boys stared at Kong's outrigger as it flashed smoothly forward. Josh sighed, feeling sick inside over what he had gotten himself into.

Manuel broke the somber silence. "I see you brought your video camera, Josh."

"I just shot some footage of Kong."

"Good!" Manuel said. "We can all study it later to see if we can spot a weakness in Kong's crew."

The boys turned their attention back to Kong. Josh again pushed the button on the camera and zoomed in for a close-up of the canoe. The front end of the boat curved up a little, like a bird's neck stretching eagerly forward. The hull was white with red trim at the upper edge of the boat, which Manuel called the gunwales.*

Six powerfully built boys in their early teens sat single file in the narrow canoe. They wore baseball caps, shorts, and no shirts. Their brown bodies seemed to be all muscle, and their powerful arms and shoulders moved in perfect rhythm.

Manuel said quietly, "They look mighty good, but there's got to be a flaw in there somewhere. See if any of you guys can spot it."

Tank said, "Looks perfect to me!"

Manuel urged, "Look closely. Watch how they paddle. Kong's in front, paddling to his left. The guy in the second seat is behind him, paddling the opposite right-hand side. Notice that the other three paddlers are also paddling on opposite sides of each other, so no two are on the same side. Now, they'll switch sides in a minute."

"Hut!" the sharp, single-word came across the water. Josh turned to Manuel, "Did he say, 'hut'?"

Manuel nodded. "Each person paddles twelve strokes on a side. On the thirteenth stroke, Two Seat calls out, 'hut.' Everyone brings in his paddle. On the fourteenth stroke, Two Seat calls, 'hit' or 'hoe.'* That's Hawaiian for 'paddle.' Then they'll all change sides."

The command, 'Hoe,' came clearly across the water. The paddles were again plunged into the water.

"I see!" Shawn exclaimed. "That way, nobody gets tired from paddling on one side all the time. If everyone paddled on the same side, the canoe would go in a circle, right?"

"They would," Manuel agreed, "except the steersman keeps them going straight."

The boys stood quietly watching their opponents' canoe glide toward them. When Kong spotted them he stiffened. He turned his head and spoke to the crew, but Josh couldn't hear what he said.

From the canoe came the crisp command, "Power ten!"

Josh turned to Manuel. "What's that mean?"

"It means pick up the pace. Kong's going to show off for us. Watch!"

The steersman called, "One! Two! Three!" The outrigger leaped forward, skimming the calm surface of the canal with a speed Josh didn't think was possible for such a long, heavy craft.

Manuel explained, "That's what you do when you're passing another canoe or when you're in trouble."

"What kind of trouble?" Josh asked. He felt a little knot of concern start to form in the pit of his stomach.

"Oh, all kinds of things can happen. Six- to eight-foot swells. Twelve-foot breaking waves. Getting hit broadside by a wave. Things like that. In a squall, everyone keeps paddling except seats four and five. They bail."

Tank uttered a low, anguished moan. "Bail?"

Manuel replied, "Yes, a canoe can swamp when waves crash over it. But don't worry. I'll teach you all the emergency stuff you'll need to know."

"All we need to know," Tank said under his breath to Josh, "is how will we ever get out of this race alive."

Kong yelled, "Hey, you, Josh! Take da kine good pi'ture of me, Kong! Da rest you haoles you t'ink you beat Kong, huh?"

Josh's stomach felt queasy as the canoe passed with a slight hissing of water along the bow and the steady, rhythmic dipping of the broad paddles. Kong's taunting laugh came across the water.

For a moment the boys were silent. Then Shawn asked, "Are you guys ready to see the canoe my folks rented for us?"

At that moment, a car roared down the boulevard and stopped by the boys. They all turned as the driver opened the car door and yelled, "Hey, you!"

Josh exclaimed, "That's the guy! The one who gave me the package!"

The man leveled a forefinger at Josh. "Come here, fast! The rest of you, get out of here!"

"Oh, oh!" Tank whispered.

Josh swallowed hard. "It's okay," he said. "You guys go on to the boat house. I'll be with you in a minute."

He picked up the video camera and started walking uneasily toward the car. The man waved impatiently for Josh to hurry. He had a scary feeling he was walking right into trouble.

Chapter Five

TRAPPED!

Josh's heart beat faster as he walked toward the rusted green sedan. He had only had a brief glimpse of the diver called Rick snorkeling in the ocean. For a moment Josh didn't think it was Rick, but when he saw the man's thin face, Josh knew it was the same man. He was standing in the street beside the open driver's door.

Rick glanced nervously around, then turned hard, cold eyes on Josh.

"Hurry up, kid! I ain't got all day."

Josh stopped on the sidewalk several feet away from the man "Hi," he said uncertainly.

"You got my package?"

"Not with me."

"Get in, and let's go get it!"

Josh shook his head firmly. "I can't do that."

"Why not?"

"I don't ride with people I don't know."

"Listen, kid, if you want to stay healthy, you'll get in this car right now so we can get my package!"

45

Josh's mouth suddenly went dry, and his tongue felt thick. "Look, I'll go get your package," he said, trying not to sound scared. "Just wait here."

The man exploded with a string of oaths and took a couple of quick, threatening steps toward the boy. "You little punk! Get in this car right now."

Josh stepped backward and started to run, but the sound of a car screeching to a stop caused him to hesitate. A small black sports car pulled up to the curb a couple of blocks away.

Rick hastily got back in his car. "Listen, kid, I got to go! I'll call you soon as I can. Have that package ready for me to pick up. And don't say anything to anybody about this if you value your health. Understand?"

Josh nodded.

The thin-faced man shook his fist and raised his voice, "If anything happens to that package, kid, you're history!" He slammed the car door shut and pulled away from the curb, tires squealing.

The driver of the sports car gunned the engine and peeled off, heading straight toward Josh. He gripped the video camera and ran toward a monkeypod* tree. He ducked behind the trunk. The black car stopped near where he had been standing. *Oh, oh!* Josh thought. *He's coming after me! What should I do now?*

Suddenly, he thought of the video camera. He hoisted it to his right shoulder and turned it on. He took a half step from behind the tree so only the camera and part of his face were exposed. He aimed the camera at the sports car.

The driver was a big man in a red and yellow aloha shirt.* He started to jump out of the car but stopped and ducked back into the sports car when he saw the camera. He burned rubber pulling away from the curb at a high speed.

"Whew!" Josh breathed a sigh of relief and lowered the camera.

He saw his friends running toward him and hurried to meet them. When they met, both Rick's battered green vehicle and the black sports car were out of sight.

Tank puffed, "What happened?"

"Yeah!" Manuel added. "Both of those guys looked like they were mad enough to make pukas* in you!"

"Especially the big guy!" Shawn said. "What gives?"

Josh remembered Rick's warning about telling anybody "Sorry, guys," Josh said, "but I can't tell you. I've got to get home."

Shawn protested, "Don't you want to see the canoe?"

"Yes, but—"

"Come on," Shawn said, turning toward the boat house "It'll only take a minute!"

Manuel and Shawn led the way. Josh deliberately slowed his pace, motioning for Tank to join him.

Tank lowered his voice. "What happened?"

Josh kept his voice down as he explained.

Tank said, "That was quick thinking, using the camera

to scare the guy off. Do you think he could recognize you?"

"I doubt it. I don't think he could see me behind the camera and the tree."

"Who was the guy in the sports car?"

"I don't know. When I get home, I'll put this cassette on the video recorder and play it back. I'd like to see that big guy's face on the screen."

"Maybe his license plate will show, too."

"I hadn't thought of that! If it does, Dad will know how to trace it through his contacts with the police."

"Josh, what do you suppose is in that package that's so important to those two guys?"

Josh shrugged. "Could be anything. Boy! I'll sure be glad to get rid of it! When we finish looking at the canoe, I'm going home and wait for Rick's call."

"I'll go with you."

Inside the boat house, Shawn limped toward a sleek canoe that was resting off the floor on boat stands. "Isn't she a beauty?" he asked, running his hand across the hull.

"It sure is!" Manuel replied. "Fiberglass, so it's lighter."

Josh walked around the outrigger canoe with mixed emotions. He felt a rising excitement at the thought of racing the sleek craft, and yet he knew his chances of beating Kong were slim. From what Grandma and Manuel had said, it wasn't just the bully who posed a threat. The unpredictable sea, possible stormy weather, and their own lack of experience were big hindrances to winning the race.

Manuel carefully checked out the craft's features, then said, "This canoe looks good all around. Good color combination, too. Most outriggers are painted the canoe club or high school colors, but this blue hull with white gunwales* is special."

Tank asked in his slow, easy manner, "What does gunwales mean?"

Manuel explained, "It means the upper edge of the boat. In the old days, I understand guns were mounted there, which is how it got its name."

Shawn peered into the canoe. "I don't see any life jackets."

Manuel smiled. "You don't wear any; you just have on a baseball cap, T-shirt and shorts."

"No shoes?" Josh asked.

Manuel shook his head. "No shoes. Oh, you could wear rubber slippers into the canoe, then kick them off and go barefooted. It's always strange to see rubber slippers floating in the canoe."

"Water is in the canoe?" Shawn asked in surprise.

"There's always a little, unless you get swamped—"

"Whoa!" Tank groaned. "I've learned all I want to know for today."

"Yeah, and I have to get home," Josh added.

The boys turned and started out of the boat house. As they walked through the doorway, Josh saw Kong and his five crew members. They had stopped their outrigger canoe near the boat ramp. They were dipping their oars into the water, scooping up something and throwing them at each other.

"What're they doing?" Josh asked Manuel. A clear, gloppy object flew from the end of Kong's paddle toward another crew member.

"They're throwing jellyfish."

Josh turned in disbelief to face Manuel. "Jellyfish?"

"That's right. They don't sting like Portuguese man-of-war do."

"But aren't jellyfish living creatures?" Josh asked.

"Sure are," Manuel answered. "Jellyfish drift along with the currents. They're pretty to see when you're swimming alongside them."

Josh felt a sadness at the senseless destruction of the defenseless creatures.

Josh called, "Hey, Kong! Stop that!"

Kong turned his massive head and glared at the four boys standing on the shore. "You going to make me?"

Josh didn't answer, knowing he had no way of doing that.

Kong's mocking laughter came across the water. "Twenty-nine moh days! Kong whip you guys, then I t'row jellyfish in you faces, yeah?"

Josh turned away. His blue eyes were hard and his voice firm as he looked at Tank, Manuel and Shawn. "We've got to beat him—somehow!"

"But how?" Tank asked.

Josh shrugged but didn't answer. Tank's words echoed in his mind as the four boys walked away from the boat house. *How? How? How?* Aloud he said, "We'll find a way. Well, I've got to get back to the apartment."

Tank said, "Me, too. See you guys later."

At the apartment, Tank and Josh climbed the stairs to Josh's apartment. The front door was locked. "Nobody home," Josh observed.

He unlocked the door, and the two friends walked barefoot across the carpet toward the videocassette recorder. Josh was removing the tape from the camera when the phone rang.

"Here," Josh handed the camera to Tank. "That's probably Rick."

"Let's hope so. Get rid of that package!"

Josh scooped up the receiver. "Hello?"

"Bring the package and meet me inside of Diamond Head* in an hour."

Josh was startled that there was no greeting. He started to ask, "Which level—" But the voice on the other end of the line cut him off.

"Come alone!"

"I can't do—" Josh exclaimed, but the phone clicked dead.

Tank asked, "What was that all about?"

Josh explained what the man said.

"You sure it was Rick?"

"I thought so," Josh answered with doubt.

"What're you going to do?"

Josh took a deep breath, his mind spinning. "First, I'll see if I can find Mom."

Josh checked a yellow note attached to the refrigerator door by a magnet shaped like a surfboard. He skimmed his mother's note:

Went shopping with Grandma, Tiffany, Nathan, Barbara and Marsha. Be back about 2 p.m. Make yourself a sandwich. Love, Mom

Josh turned to Tank. "I'd better call Dad at the paper."

A moment later he said, "This is Josh Ladd. May I speak to my father, please?"

"I'm sorry, Josh," the woman said. Her voice had a slight rising inflection at the end. "Your father went to see an advertising client."

"When will he be back?"

"Late," the woman answered. "May I take a message?"

"I guess not," Josh hesitated then said. "It would be too late. Thanks anyway."

When he hung up, he turned to Tank. "Dad's not there."

"What're you going to do?"

Josh thought for a moment. "I've got no choice! I've got to take that package and meet Rick like he said."

"Alone?" There was alarm in his friend's voice.

"But that could be dangerous, especially if that other

big guy follows Rick."

"I know! But Rick found me at the Ala Wai Canal,* so he'll surely find me here or someplace else. Not showing up at Diamond Head won't solve my problem. I've got to get the package back to that diver."

"I still think you should open it, and see why it's so important that those two guys want it."

"It's not mine to open. Well, I'd better get the package and go to Diamond Head. Trouble is, Rick didn't say where to meet him."

"That's crazy. That dead volcano has several floors inside it."

"Yeah, I know," answered Josh. "How many times have we explored it?"

"Lots!" Tank followed Josh into his bedroom. "Then how will you find this Rick guy?"

"I guess he'll have to find me."

"I don't like it, Josh! You know how dark and spooky that place is!"

Josh opened the closet door. "I know."

"I'll come with you!"

Josh pulled the package down from where he had hidden it on the shelf and tied it to his belt. "You can't! Rick said I had to come alone."

"Then I'll follow you. Maybe Rick'll think I'm just another kid playing around in there. If you get in trouble, I'll be there to help."

"I don't know, Tank. It could be dangerous."

"That's why I need to go with you. It can't be anymore dangerous for two of us, can it?"

"I guess not," Josh said. "We'd better wear our tennis shoes and bring flashlights."

A half hour later, with only a casual glance backward to make sure Tank was following at a safe distance, Josh walked alone into the opening at the side of Diamond Head.

Unknown to many visitors, the inside of the dead volcano was honeycombed with tunnels. They had been carved out years before and used during World War II. Now the tunnels were dark and gloomy. They had a damp, mildewy odor. No light penetrated the tunnels, except at each level where rusted metal ladders pushed through holes to the next floor. Shafts of sunlight also revealed huge metal gun mounts where heavy artillery had once pointed seaward.

Josh flipped on his flashlight. *Whoops,* he thought, *the batteries are weak.* He checked to make sure the package was still tied to the belt at his waist. He stepped onto the iron ladder carefully and climbed down, listening for any voices or movement. He stayed close to the ladders; he didn't want to stray inside the tunnels. Josh whistled to let Rick know where he was and to cover his own fears. The ragged, uncertain sound of his whistling echoed through the tunnels.

About ten minutes later, Josh thought he heard a sound in the dark tunnel behind him. He stopped whistling and listened intently. Slowly he turned around, hanging on to the ladder with one hand, while with his other hand he pointed the flashlight into the tunnel. The weak beam flickered. A big, brown rat ran, squeaking from the light, and disappeared in the darkness.

Josh sighed with relief, sucked in his breath and held it to listen again. He heard someone coming down the metal ladder from the floor above him. Whoever it was moved quietly, making only the faintest sounds as his hands and feet left one rusted rung for the next.

Josh started to call, "Rick, is that you?" Then he heard other footsteps behind him in the darkened tunnel.

Oh, no! he thought in sudden panic. *Two people are coming! One must be Rick. But who's the other one? What if it's the big guy who's been chasing Rick? I'm trapped between them!*

Chapter Six

A CHASE IN THE DARK

Josh held his breath, turning his head rapidly so he could see both the iron ladder above him and the concrete tunnel behind him. No sound came from the underground passageway behind him, but someone was definitely coming down the ladder. A small light glowed faintly, showing a man's foot slowly feeling for the rung below. Josh stood in the tunnel and watched the faint glow from a flashlight shine on a man's foot that was stepping down on the next rung. It was a big foot in a Roman sandal.

The boy nervously fingered the package still tied to his waistband. His heart thumped hard.

Both sandaled feet stopped abruptly on the rusted iron rungs. The man's chest and head were out of view, but he had on a pair of cutoff shorts. "That you, kid?" The voice echoed in the smelly concrete tunnel.

"It's. . .it's me. . .Josh Ladd." His voice was weak and a little squeaky.

"Good!" The man's voice echoed eerily in the concrete

passageway. "Come over to the ladder, turn off your light, and hand the package up to me."

Josh couldn't tell if it was Rick's voice. He started to hand the package up to the man, but when he looked at his big muscular legs, an uneasy feeling came over Josh. *Rick's not a big man,* he thought.

Aloud Josh said, "I . . . I can't give it to you!" The boy tipped the light up slightly, trying to see the man's face.

"Turn that light down and hand up the package fast!" The man's hand dropped into view. His big fingers motioned impatiently.

Josh felt a tingling sensation start along his shoulders and ripple down his arms, leaving goose bumps. "No! You're not the one who gave it to me!" He announced his decision so firmly he startled himself.

An explosive swear word made the boy jump back. "Okay, kid! You asked for it!" The left foot moved quickly down the ladder rung.

Josh spun around, ready to run for his life. But which way? The shortest way out was behind him, but he had heard someone back there. Having explored the tunnels with Tank, Josh knew that a short distance ahead there were more rusted ladders. These led both up and down to other levels in the volcano. There was also one of several Y's in the underground passage that branched off in two directions.

In most of the Y's it didn't matter which tunnel Josh took. They all eventually led to other ladders. But the Y ahead was different. One branch led to iron ladders and safety. The other branch ended at a chain link and barbed wire fence with warning signs:

Keep Out! U.S. Military Property!

If Josh made a wrong turn and ended up at the fence, he couldn't escape the angry man clambering quickly down the ladder. As one of the big man's sandals touched the tunnel floor, Josh decided. He didn't want to face whatever unseen person lurked in the shadows behind him, so Josh sprinted ahead. He ran so fast his flashlight's weak beam barely showed him the way.

"I'll get you, kid!" The big man's roar filled the tunnel. The bright beam from his flashlight caught Josh from behind.

Josh panted as he drove his body forward as fast as possible. He rounded a curve in the damp, stinky tunnel. *The* Y! *Which way?*

Josh couldn't recall. Desperately racing toward the point where the tunnels branched off, he tried to remember.

Left or right? Josh searched his mind, panic making the decision harder. *Right! That's the way out! No! Left! It's left! No!...*"

Puffing hard, the boy dashed toward the Y. His mind tumbled with indecision. He reached the point where the passageway went in two directions, but he still wasn't sure. *I'll try right! If I'm wrong, I've had it!*

He dashed into the tunnel to the right. Behind him,

he heard a triumphant roar. "Now I've got you!"

"He knows the tunnel! I made a mistake!" Josh moaned, "I've got to turn back and take the other. . . .Too late!"

His pursuer was gaining on Josh. Josh speeded up again. He felt a stitch developing in his side. His lungs hurt from running so hard. His weak flashlight beam reflected off the heavy, chain link fence. He groaned, "Trapped!"

Josh looked frantically around for a military man who might be patrolling in a jeep or on foot, but nobody was in sight. Josh heard the heavy thudding of his pursuer, closing in fast.

He slowed at the fence and shone his flashlight upward. Vicious coils of barbed wire curled across the top of the chain-link fence.

Josh's mind screamed. *He's got me unless I can get by him!*

Josh spun around and crouched to face the onrushing man. The man's powerful light momentarily blinded the boy. Josh's breath came in ragged gulps. In a moment, he would have to run again—if he managed to slip by the man when he grabbed for Josh.

"Stand still and give me the package!" The big man's voice roared in the tunnel.

Josh's body was tight as a bowstring about to release an arrow. He nodded weakly, puffing hard. Then he started to reach for his waistband. The man's light followed

Josh's hand movements. The light had blinded Josh, and he blinked as he tried to see the man. If he didn't get past the man now, it would be too late.

Now! Josh leaped forward and struck at the man's flashlight. It sailed crazily through the air, making weird shadows on the ceiling and walls.

"What the—?" the man's startled cry exploded from his lips. Josh heard a heavy hand whoosh past his ear; then the boy dodged past the man. The man's flashlight crashed against the concrete wall and went out.

Good! Josh thought. Forcing his tired body to keep moving, he ran as hard as before. His eyes followed the ever-weakening beam of his flashlight. *My batteries are about gone! I've got to find a ladder before they go dead!*

Behind him, he heard the big man swearing angrily. Josh guessed he was feeling for the flashlight Josh had knocked out of his hand.

He found it, Josh realized, for the man gave a triumphant shout when his flashlight winked on. The pursuer, yelling with anger, started after the boy again.

Where's the nearest ladder? Josh thought. He wasn't sure where he was in the tunnels.

A painful fire burned in his chest. Each breath he took seared like a hot iron. He was slowing, too, his energy quickly draining. *If I make another mistake, he'll get me for sure!*

Josh stumbled slightly as he approached the Y. *Better go straight ahead the way I came in,* he decided. *I just hope I can keep going until I get out of here!*

He stumbled and almost fell as he approached the other tunnel. "Lord, help me!" Josh prayed. It was one prayer he had offered before in his young life, but right now he meant it with all his heart.

The big man was gaining; Josh heard his thundering steps coming closer and closer. Josh thought, *I'm not going to make it!*

He came to the Y where the tunnel separated again into two passages. The flashlight's pale glow caught a movement just ahead of him. Someone was pressed flat against the wall at the junction of the tunnels.

Josh veered away, stumbling over his own tired feet. He started to fall forward and thrust out his left hand to break his fall. He tried to hold on to the light with his right hand.

Josh fought to regain his balance but fell to his knees. The rough concrete floor tore into his free hand and both knees. He tried to ignore the pain. He leaped up, still clutching the flashlight, but it was too late.

Josh's pursuer was upon him, reaching out with the flashlight just inches away. "Got you!"

Josh cringed, expecting powerful hands to clamp down hard on him. Instead, the big man tripped and staggered forward.

Startled, Josh turned in time to see the flying light reveal another man's foot and leg. Josh realized the man hiding against the wall had tripped Josh's pursuer. The big man fell face-first, his hands in front of him. He let out a startled, painful, "Oof!"

Then his flashlight crashed against the floor front-end-down. Josh heard the tinkle of breaking glass, and the light winked out.

He staggered forward, too weary even to wonder who had helped him. He reached the first metal ladder just as his own flashlight went out. He dropped it and scrambled up the rungs.

As he burst into full sunlight, Tank rushed up. "Josh! What happened? Look at your hands and knees."

Josh was out of breath, and he hurt so much from exertion he couldn't talk.

Tank bent beside Josh. "I tried to follow you, but I lost you in the tunnel. Did you meet Rick and give him the package?"

Josh shook his head and tapped his waistband.

"You've still got it?"

"Yes."

"Then you've still got big trouble!"

"Don't say that!" Josh added. "We better get out of here."

The boys started down the outside of the volcano toward their apartment building. As Josh regained his breath, he told Tank what had happened. When Josh finished, Tank looked at him with troubled eyes.

"Do you think it was Rick who tripped the guy chasing you?"

"I didn't see him, so I don't know. I have a funny feeling there was somebody else in that tunnel—a third person. But who?"

"That's a spooky thought, Josh."

Josh took a slow, deep breath and let it out. "Well, whether it was only Rick and the big guy, or if there was a third person in there, I'm still stuck with the package."

Tank asked softly, "What're you going to do?"

"I'm going to tell my Dad."

"Rick warned you not to tell anybody."

"I know, but I'm going to tell my father, anyway."

"You could open the package first."

Josh shook his head. "No. It's not my package." He looked down at his bloody hand and knees. "Let's get back to the apartment and clean up these cuts so they don't get infected."

As the boys approached their apartments, Tank suggested, "We had better come up with some ideas of where we're going to get the other two paddlers we need for the race."

"Yeah," Josh sighed. "If we don't find someone right away we'll have to let our sisters help, and that'll give Kong a big laugh. We'll find somebody," Josh said firmly. "We've just got to!"

He was right, but it would happen in a most unexpected way.

Chapter Seven

A STRANGE DISAPPEARANCE

When Josh's father arrived home from work, the boy sat in one of the big occasional chairs. Josh repeated what he had already told the rest of his family about his scary experiences inside the old volcano. Josh still ached from the cuts and bruises he had gotten when he fell.

John Ladd fingered the package thoughtfully while Josh explained how he got it. He told the whole story about the phone call, being warned by Kong, encountering Rick, taking video footage of the big guy in the sports car and finally being chased in the tunnel.

"What do you think I should do, Dad?" Josh finished "Shall I open the package?"

His father shook his head. "First, let's put that videocassette on to see what you got at the Ala Wai Canal."*

All six Ladd family members waited quietly, watching for the video pictures to appear on the TV screen. Josh found his heart speeding up as he watched the big man's sports car zoom up to the curb.

"Here's where I hid behind the tree and began shooting the pictures," Josh explained. "See how the driver ducked back inside the car?"

"Can't make out the license plate," Mr. Ladd said. "It looks like it has something over it."

As John Ladd rewound the tape, Grandma made little clucking sounds. "I don't like this a bit! Not a bit. Joshua, you may be in real danger."

"Yes," Mary Ladd said. "Why didn't you tell us about this sooner? You could have been seriously hurt by those men."

"I know," Josh replied, with a worried look on his face. "I didn't think too much about it when the guy gave me the package. I thought I could give it back to him on the cat' and everything would be okay. But I knew I'd better tell you and Dad after that guy chased me."

Nathan exclaimed, "Maybe that guy will come in the night and sneak in our bedroom and—"

"Nathan!" his father interrupted. Mr. Ladd walked over and put his arm around Nathan. "You're a wonderful son, but I do wish you would not express such terrible thoughts."

Josh tried to ignore the seed of fear Nathan had planted "What are you going to do now, Dad?"

Josh's mother suggested, "Why not call the police and let them decide what to do?"

"There's something else we might do first, Mary. Josh,

you said this man Rick found you through Kong. Do you have his number?"

"Kong's?" Josh almost choked at the idea. "Why would I want his number? I wish he were on another planet!"

"Now, Son!" his father chided gently. He carried the package to the telephone and picked up the directory. "Let's see if his parents are listed. Do you know their first names?"

"No, but Kong lives with his mother on the next street over, so maybe you can find it by the address."

A moment later Mr. Ladd peered over the top of his silver framed half glasses and said, "This must be it." He dialed while the family sat anxiously waiting.

"No answer," Mr. Ladd announced in a moment. "Well, Son, if you don't mind, I'll keep this package until I decide what we're going to do."

"Fine with me!" Josh said. "I've had enough troubles with it to last me a long time."

"Now," his father continued, standing. "It's time you kids got ready for bed. I don't want to be late for Sunday school tomorrow."

The next morning, the Ladd family's station wagon pulled into the parking lot at the neighborhood community church. The grounds were covered with a colored rainbow of flowering plants. The walkways were lined with hibiscus,* Hawaii's state flower. On a coral wall, cut from beneath the sea by Hawaiian divers, bougainvillea* grew in heavy clusters of coral, purple and white.

Tank's family had arrived earlier, so he pushed himself away from the gray trunk of a royal palm and hurried to meet Josh. After the boys greeted each other, they headed to their Sunday school class while Josh updated Tank on what he had told his parents the night before.

Everyone, including the Ladds and Catletts, was dressed informally. The men and boys wore cool aloha shirts* outside their light pants. The boys wore sandals instead of zoris. The women and girls had on cotton dresses or brightly patterned muumuus.*

As Josh and Tank entered their class, they stopped in surprise. Two new boys were taking seats near the front of the room.

"Wow!" Josh whispered, leaning close to Tank's ear "Look at the size of those kanakas!"*

"Yeah! Are you thinking what I'm thinking?"

"They didn't get those muscles from playing with marbles! Let's ask them if they would like to join our canoe team!"

Mr. Valderama, a small Filipino man who taught their class, raised his voice to get the boys' attention. "Take seat, please!"

Although English was used in the Philippine Islands, some people who had migrated from there to Hawaii spoke with an accent. Mr. Valderama had a slightly lilting voice, and he tended to drop words from his sentences when he spoke. "We have kamaaina* visitors from Big Island."

Josh and Tank exchanged knowing glances. Tank whispered, "From the Big Island! That means they're probably experienced in paddling canoes!"

Mr. Valderama continued, pointing a short, stubby brown finger at the two newcomers. "This is Kala* and Koma* Lama. You already meet parents. Been visitors here past weeks. Sons just back from living on Mainland. All join church today."

Tank leaned over and anxiously whispered to Josh, "If they've been on the Mainland, maybe they've forgotten how to paddle!"

"Not likely, but let's grab them at the break and find out."

At the coffee hour between Sunday school and church, Josh and Tank rushed up to the big kanakas. Before the friends could say anything, the church membership chairwoman came bustling over to the Lama brothers. She hurried them off to meet with their parents and the pastor for last minute instructions. Reluctantly, Tank and Josh took seats in the church and waited. Dr. Chin entered in his flowing black robes.

"Aloha nui,"* Dr. Chin began from the pulpit, flashing his usual warm smile. His salt-and-pepper hair was cut short. He raised his hand and said with a wave, "Welcome to the worship service. Let's begin by standing and singing 'Ke Mele Hoomaikai,* Song of Praise.' Please remain standing for the Lord's Prayer, which we will say together, each in his own language. For those of you who would like the Hawaiian words, they are printed in the bulletin."

After the opening Song of Praise, Josh and Tank felt good as they looked at the prospective canoers. The two friends recited the Lord's Prayer in Hawaiian. It began, "E Ko Makou Makua Iloko O Ka Lani...."*

At the close of the service, the new members were called forward. Josh and Tank grinned at each other as Kala and Koma Lama and their parents arose from their seats.

Dr. Chin conducted the customary membership service. When he placed fragrant Hawaiian leis* about the necks of the four members, he hugged them the aloha* way. After the benediction, Josh and Tank were the first in line to greet the Lama family.

"Hi," Josh said when it came his turn to meet the oldest boy. "I'm Josh Ladd."

"Yeah, and I'm Tank Catlett."

"I'm Koma, but most kids call me Big K." He jerked his head toward his brother standing beside him. "He's called Little K."

Josh said, "Boy, are we glad you came to our church! When Tank and I saw you this morning, we thought you might join our crew. You guys ever paddle an outrigger canoe?"

Big K smiled down at Josh. "We were born in one." He turned both palms upward. "See these calluses? They come from using a paddle so long. My kid brother, too." He indicated the boy beside him. "Why? Do you belong to a canoe club?"

"Well, no, but my friend Tank and I are involved in a little race, and we're looking for a couple of good paddlers."

"You found them!" Big K reached over and punched his brother in the shoulder. "Canoe race," he said, jerking his head toward Josh and Tank.

"Great!" Little K replied with a big smile. "When can we talk?"

"Meet us in the parking lot by the first royal palm as soon as you're through here!" Josh answered.

Outside by the royal palm tree, Tank said, "You and I are big for our ages, but those two kanakas are nearly as big as this tree!"

"They'll make a great engine for the canoe!" Josh agreed.

A little while later the Lama brothers came outside to meet with Josh and Tank. After they had talked for awhile, Tank asked, "Are you pure-blooded Hawaiians?"

"Not many of those left, if any," Big K answered. "We're hapa haole,* half white—mostly German, English and Irish. The rest is Hawaiian, Samoan, Japanese and maybe a little Chinese."

"Yeah, we're your typical Hawaiians," Little K added "Now, tell us about this canoe race."

Josh and Tank excitedly told them everything, from Shawn's challenge by Kong to the rented canoe they had for the race. Josh concluded, "Now that we've got you two to help paddle, we can begin practicing."

The boys exchanged phone numbers and parted. Josh and Tank were almost floating across the church grounds to their family cars. On the drive back to the apartment, Josh jabbered so excitedly about the new paddlers that everyone caught the excitement, except Tiffany.

"It's not fair!" she said from the back seat where she sat between her two brothers. "Marsha and I deserve a chance to be in that race. It's not right to keep us out just because we're girls!"

Josh said, "We don't need you any more, Tif! We've got Big K and Little K!"

Mr. Ladd cleared his throat and eased the station wagon around a corner. "I'm glad you've got your other paddlers, Josh, but I think it's only fair that Tiffany and Marsha at least be allowed to participate as relief paddlers."

Josh started to protest, then shrugged. He thought, *We won't need any relief paddlers, but it'll be okay for Tif and Marsha to ride in the Boston Whaler and think they're going to be in the race.* Aloud, the boy said, "That's okay by me. I think the other boys will agree, too, after I explain it to them."

"Good!" Mr. Ladd replied. "Now, let's get home and call Kong's number again. I want to see if he knows how to get in touch with Rick so we can return his package."

At the apartment, Mr. Ladd dialed while the family watched expectantly. "Mrs. Kong? I'm your neighbor,

John Ladd. Your son, what? Oh, no! No! I'm not calling to complain!

"A day or so ago, your son delivered a message to my son, Josh, from a man named Rick. We don't know the man's last name. But it's important that we reach him. Do you know his phone number or last name? What?" Mr. Ladd nodded and listened. "Okay, thank you," he said, with a puzzled look on his face as he hung up the phone receiver.

"Dad, what is it?" asked Josh.

"She says Kong is out helping look for Rick."

"Looking for him?" Josh exclaimed. "Why?"

"Because he's disappeared!"

Chapter Eight

SOMEBODY'S WATCHING

The family buzzed with excitement after Mr. Ladd finished his conversation with Kong's mother. He turned to face everyone. "She says this fellow Rick was supposed to meet Kong yesterday morning but didn't. In the afternoon, some other friends called to say Rick wasn't home, and they couldn't find him. When Kong checked again this morning and nobody had seen Rick, Kong and some of his friends went to look for him."

Nathan exclaimed, "I bet I know what happened! That big guy who chased Josh probably took Rick out to sea and—"

"Nathan!" Mr. and Mrs. Ladd spoke the word together, interrupting their youngest son's explanation.

Nathan turned to Josh and whispered, "I'll bet you'll be next!"

"Now, Nathan," his father said with strained patience, "your brother's not going to be harmed. Josh, please go to our bedroom. Bring the package that Rick gave you to keep. It's right on top of our dresser."

73

Josh started down the hallway, asking over his shoulder, "Are you going to open it?"

"No, I'm going to call the police and let them do that."

Josh hurried into his parents' bedroom and checked the dresser top. Josh raised his voice. "Dad, I don't see it."

"It's right in plain sight, Son. You can't miss it!"

Josh looked again and then called, "I still don't see it."

"All right, I'll come get it myself."

Mr. Ladd entered the room with his usual long-legged stride. "It's right...Hmm!" He looked over at the bedside tables, then exclaimed, "It's gone! Did anyone pick up that package?"

The other family members claimed no one had touched it. During a careful search of the apartment, Nathan let out a cry. "Hey, Dad! This lock's broken!" He pointed at the lanai* door.

The other five family members gathered around to examine the latch. Mr. Ladd muttered, "It was skillfully done, so whoever did it knew exactly what he was doing. At least the package was out in the open, so he didn't ransack the place."

Nathan looked up at his big brother. "See how easy he got in? Maybe you'd better not sleep in our room in case he shows up again tonight."

"Nathan," Mr. Ladd said firmly, "that's enough of your scary imagination! The thief has no reason to return because he got what he wanted. Now I'd like each of you to go around to the neighbors. Ask if they saw anybody suspicious. Report back before the police arrive."

When everyone returned from checking with the neighbors, no one had any helpful information except for Josh. "I talked to Roger's grandmother," he told the family. "She's coming downstairs as soon as she changes clothes. She didn't want to talk to a policeman in her housedress."

Josh started to explain what he had learned from Roger's grandmother when someone knocked at the door. A uniformed haole* policeman and a Japanese-American in plainclothes were standing outside.

Mr. Ladd introduced himself and opened the door. The taller man said, "I'm Detective Sergeant Tomashima. This is Officer York." Both of them removed their shoes before entering the apartment.

John Ladd summarized all that had happened, including Josh's being handed a package off Molokini,* the chase in the tunnel and the disappearance of the package.

The officers examined the lanai door and confirmed that the break-in was professional. The detective asked, "How did the suspect know where to find the package without tearing this place apart?"

"It was on top of the dresser," Mr. Ladd said.

Josh said, "Here comes our upstairs neighbor, Mrs. Yamaguchi. Maybe she can help answer your questions."

Roger Okamoto's maternal grandmother was a small, slender woman with gray streaks in her hair. She removed her wooden sandals and nervously entered the room. She acknowledged the introduction to the policemen with a slight bow.

Josh urged, "Mrs. Yamaguchi, tell these policemen what you told me."

She nodded. "Yess, I exprain." She made a slightly hissing sound on the final 's' and said 'r' for an 'l' sound.

The elderly woman said she had been alone in the Okamotos' third-floor apartment about ten o'clock that morning. Almost everyone was away, so the apartment complex was quiet. She heard a noise and looked down from the lanai. "Big haole man," she concluded, raising her right hand high above her own five-foot height, "lun 'way fast." She pointed down the apartment driveway toward the main street. "Not see face."

Josh suddenly thought of something. "Did he wear Roman sandals and no socks?"

"Ah, yesss! Same!"

Josh thought of something else. "Dad, could we show her and the policeman the video I took of the man who chased me? Make sure it's the same person?"

"Good idea, Son!" Mr. Ladd hurried to set up the video recorder and turned on the cassette.

When the television screen showed the big man start to get out of the black sports car, Mrs. Yamaguchi let out a little exclamation. "Rarry!" she cried.

The entire Ladd family and the officers looked at the elderly woman. She wagged her right finger in recognition and repeated, "Rarry!" Mrs. Yamaguchi smiled. "Not know rast name. Visit sometime." She pointed to the adjacent apartment building about forty feet away.

Josh nodded with satisfaction. "His name's Larry, and he visits somebody in the other building, so he knows this neighborhood."

Mr. Ladd agreed. "He could have been visiting someone in a nearby apartment. When he saw us leave for church this morning, he broke into our place."

The officers took Mrs. Yamaguchi's statement and then the three left. Josh looked at his father. "Do you think they'll catch him?"

Mr. Ladd shook his head with doubt. "I'm not too hopeful. Except for the break-in, there's really been no crime. Nothing's missing but the package. Since we don't know what's in it, we don't know if it's valuable or not. Those officers have so many important cases, this one won't have much of a priority."

"What about Rick's disappearing?"

"Unless someone reports a person missing, the police can't do anything. So far, nobody's turned in a report on Rick. Except for the burglary, I would guess this case is closed. Anyway, the package is gone, so that should be the end of that. Now we can all forget about it and concentrate on the canoe race."

Josh wasn't so sure that this was the end of the case. He was still anxious, even after Sergeant Tomashima later reported that routine checks of the neighborhood had failed to find anybody who knew Larry's last name or whom he visited in the apartment complex.

Josh learned from one of Kong's friends that Rick was still missing, but that someone else reported that Rick was vacationing on the Mainland. Nobody was looking for him anymore.

"Everybody acts as if I should forget about Rick and the package," Josh complained to Tank, Roger, Manuel, Shawn and Big and Little K a couple of days later as they met for their first canoe practice. Josh told them the whole story and then said, "But I don't feel it's over at all. In fact, I feel like that guy we read about with the sword hanging over his head."

"That was Damocles,"* Manuel said. "Remember? It's a legend about a man named Damocles. He was happy until one time at a banquet he looked up and saw a sword hanging over his head suspended by a single hair."

Josh nodded. "That's how I'll feel until I know what happened with Rick and Larry."

"Aw," Tank scoffed, "the package is gone, so you've got nothing to worry about, except practicing racing canoes so we can beat Kong!"

Josh asked, "What happens if Rick shows up and wants his package?"

"Forget it!" Tank urged.

But Josh couldn't drive away the fear that Rick would show up again.

Shawn changed the subject. "Let's get going! The first thing we have to figure out is who sits where in the canoe."

"Yeah," Tank agreed. "At first we didn't have enough

paddlers; now we've got too many. At least it'll keep our sisters from bugging us about being in the race."

Josh suggested, "Tank, Shawn and I have no experience, so we've got to rely on you four guys." Josh turned toward Manuel, Roger, and Big and Little K. "Where do you think each one of us should be in the canoe?"

Roger replied, "Since I'm not in the race, I'll be the trainer and ride in the Boston Whaler. We'll still have one extra guy, so how about taking turns as relief paddlers and ride in the whaler with the driver and me?"

That was agreeable, except nobody wanted to give up a seat in the outrigger. Finally Josh announced, "I'll ride in the powerboat and trade with anybody in any seat for a while. Okay?"

"Yeah," Tank teased. "You can be with Tiffany and Marsha!"

"Don't laugh!" Josh warned as the other boys chuckled. "My father and Tank's father both agreed that unless the girls are allowed to train as relief paddlers, Tank and I can't be in the race."

Manuel said, "It'll make it harder for Josh to trade places with someone in the canoe if we don't let the sisters trade off, too. But we'll think about that later. For now, do we agree that Roger is the coach?"

The boys nodded.

Roger said, "Manuel, you'd better take Seat Two because you're experienced and know how to call the rowing changes. We need Big and Little K in the engine positions because of their strength. So, Big K, how about taking Seat Three and Little K Seat Four?"

The Lama brothers agreed, but Shawn limped over to Roger and asked, "Hey, how about me? I'm the one who accepted Kong's challenge and got my father to rent us a canoe, you know!"

Roger nodded, "I'm getting to you, but that gives us a problem. You probably want Seat One. He sets the pace, and you're inexperienced."

Shawn added, "That's true, but I'm not asking you to give me any special consideration because of this leg." He slapped his left thigh. "I'll learn fast and earn the right to that first seat!"

"Okay," Roger agreed. "We'll try it. So we've got Seats One, Two, Three and Four settled. Seat Five should be another strong person. The idea is to put everyone where he'll do the best job."

Tank suggested, "Let Josh and me try Seat Five. We'll trade off."

Roger nodded, "Let's try it. That leaves only the steersman. He's got to be experienced to keep the canoe on course. In fact, the sixth man is the key member of the race, but we don't have anyone who's qualified."

Josh, usually the leader in any situation, had let Roger take over. Now Josh suggested, "You're qualified, Roger."

"Huh-uh! I already told you I won't be in the race! I've had enough trouble with Kong!"

Josh asked, "If you're the trainer, won't Kong think

you're one of the racing crew?"

Roger was silent a moment before answering. "Guess you're right. Okay, if I'm the steersman, then who's going to be the trainer and ride in the powerboat?"

Josh suggested, "We won't have any. Why don't you and Manuel coach us from the canoe? Okay with all the rest of you?"

"Sure." "Great!" the boys said in agreement.

Josh smiled. "Okay, then it's settled. Now, what do we do first?"

Roger said, "We'll start with the basics and practice before we get in the canoe. Everybody line up single file the way you'll sit in the outrigger."

When this was done, each boy was handed a paddle. Roger explained, "This is made of laminated wood, and it's about fifty inches long. Place your left hand across the top."

Manuel broke in, "That's called the *teetop* because of its shape."

"Right," Roger agreed. "There's a correct way to hold it. Your right hand goes above the blade about six inches. Now, Manuel, you show them what to do when you give your commands."

Manuel extended his paddle out to the left. "When I call, 'reach out,' Seat One—that's you, Shawn—always starts by extending his paddle to the left side. Seat Two does the opposite, holding his paddle to the right and so on down the line. That way, the person sitting closest to you is stroking on the opposite side.

"Each crew member paddles twelve strokes on a side. I'll count them to myself," Manuel continued to explain. "On the thirteenth stroke, I'll call 'hut.' Pull your paddles out of the water. When I say 'hoe'* or 'hit,' put your paddles back into the water on the opposite side."

Roger added, "The big problem here is to keep from clobbering the person ahead of you with your paddle. Now, let's try it before we get in the canoe."

Paddling in the air seemed strange to Josh. He nearly burst out laughing at Manuel's cry of 'hut!' Tank eagerly lifted his paddle and swung it to the other side, whacking Little K in the middle of his broad shoulders.

"Hey!" the big kaamaina* cried, turning around to face Tank. "You do that again, I'll trade places with you and show you how that smarts!"

"Sorry," Tank apologized. "I'll watch it."

"Okay, guys," Roger said, "let's try it again."

The boys continued practicing paddling in the air until loud laughter exploded behind them. Everyone spun around.

Kong stood with hands on hips, a big grin splitting his face. "Pupule,* all of you. Paddle on da kine* dry land! Kong beat all you easy foh shuh!"

As he turned away, laughing, the boys silently looked after him. Josh glanced at their faces and saw doubt. He whispered hoarsely, "Don't listen to him, you guys! We're going to give him a surprise on race day!"

The other boys nodded and voiced their agreement as they turned back to face Roger, their trainer. "Okay," he said, "let's try an easy forty-eight-strokes-a-minute pace. Sixty is average in racing, but we'll speed up to seventy-two. When we've practiced them all, then we'll train in the canoe."

In the midst of their exercises, Josh suddenly stopped, with his paddle in midair. He stared at a car driving by on the far side of the boulevard.

"Hey, you guys!" he exclaimed. "I thought Rick had disappeared, but I just saw him!"

Chapter Nine

ANOTHER CHALLENGE AND A SURPRISE

All paddles stopped in mid-air as their handlers turned in surprise to face Josh.

"Where?" Tank asked.

"Right over there!" Josh pointed. "See that car just turning the corner? That was Rick."

Tank scoffed. "It couldn't have been!"

"I tell you, that's who it was. He didn't see me, but I got a good look at him."

"Who's this Rick guy?" Big K asked. Lowering his paddle to the ground, he flexed his shoulders.

Josh explained, "He's the man I told you about who gave me a package to hold for him. But we think a big guy named Larry broke into our apartment and stole the package."

Roger frowned. "I thought the police figured Rick had gone to the Mainland or else that Larry character had gotten to him."

Josh licked his lips; all of a sudden his mouth seemed dry. "Well, no matter where he was, he's back. And that means he's going to be contacting me, wanting his package!"

Tank's eyes opened wide with understanding. "What's going to happen when you tell him you don't have it?"

"I . . . I don't know." Josh's voice was barely a whisper.

All the boys looked silently at Josh for a moment. Then Manuel said softly, "Josh, it looks like you were right about the sword of Damocles.* It's still hanging over you!"

Josh didn't feel like practicing with the canoe crew anymore. He and Tank walked thoughtfully back to the Ladds' apartment. When they went into the kitchen, Josh found a note on the refrigerator door.

Josh, I took Grandma, Tiffany and Nathan shopping. Be back before dinner. Love, Mom

While Tank walked from window to window, checking the parking lot and adjacent apartment area for Rick, Josh called his father at work. The receptionist said he had flown to one of the other islands on business. Josh thanked her, set the phone down and turned toward Tank.

"Help me think what I should do when Rick calls!"

"Stall! Don't tell him you don't have the package. Maybe that will give the police time to find him."

"But Rick hasn't broken any laws that I know about. The police wanted to locate him because he was reported missing. Even if they talked to him, it would only be to find out where he'd been. The man the cops want is Larry!"

"And so will Rick!" Tank left the window and plopped heavily onto the couch. "But Rick won't know that until he talks to you and learns Larry stole the package. And if Rick doesn't believe you—"

"Yeah! I could end up in real trouble!"

The rest of the day dragged on, but Rick didn't call. Josh was at a loss to explain why but Tank wasn't.

"I told you, Josh, that wasn't Rick you saw drive by. So forget it, and let's concentrate on canoeing."

When the family came home, Tank went downstairs to his apartment while Josh told his mother, grandmother, sister and brother about seeing Rick. The family all agreed that Tank was probably right; it hadn't been Rick at all, so Josh should not worry about it.

Josh tried, but that night he lay awake a long time, tense and alert, waiting for the phone to ring. He was still awake when he heard his father pad down the hallway in his house slippers.

Josh heard his father prowl the apartment, gently testing the doors and windows to be sure they were locked securely. Josh knew that the louvers, always left open to allow the trade winds to blow through, could easily be removed by someone who really wanted to break into the house. But Rick wasn't likely to do that, the boy told himself. Rick would call and want Josh to meet him with the package.

That night passed without incident; then several days and nights slid by. Whenever the phone rang, Josh jumped. Often he checked the sliding screen door on the lanai,* half expecting that Kong would call to tell him to come out so he could deliver a message from Rick. The only time Josh forgot about Rick was during the daily canoe practice. He used his video camera to shoot footage of his and Kong's crew during practice sessions to see how the teams were progressing.

Tiffany and Marsha became the relief paddlers, unaware that behind their backs the seven boys were smiling and making fun of them. The boys had no intention of ever letting the girls participate in the race.

At first, Josh and Tank allowed their sisters to take their place at Seat Five. But the two girls wanted to paddle together, so Shawn volunteered to let Marsha have his Seat One for a while.

Josh and Tank moaned and groaned in mock despair at their sisters' first awkward efforts with the paddles. The girls said they would show them and tried even harder.

One day when they were alone, Josh reluctantly admitted to Tank, "Our sisters are doing better than I expected."

"Yeah, but we can't let them in the race!"

At night, while Josh listened with half an ear for Rick to call, the other boys reviewed the day's videotapes.

After about a week without seeing Rick again or receiving any call from him, Josh began to relax a little. During practice, he stood on the banks of the Ala Wai Canal* with video camera ready as Tiffany and Marsha took their seats in the canoe for a practice run.

Just as all the crew members got settled in the outrigger, Josh saw his sister stiffen, an expression of defiance on her face. He followed her gaze. Kong and his crew members were paddling their outrigger toward them.

Josh heard Tiffany say to the other five crew members, "Let's show Kong what we can do!" She raised her voice and called, "Reach out!"

Josh was so surprised he almost dropped the video camera off his shoulder. "Girls!" he muttered to himself. "Seat One doesn't call commands. Roger the steersman, does that."

Josh got another surprise when he heard Roger echo Tiffany. "Reach out!"

The crew obeyed the command in unison. Their blades flashed like silver in the sun. The two girls' paddles seemed to be tied to the boys', for they all moved as one.

Tiffany, in the bow, poised her paddle on the left, the correct starting position for Seat One. Each of the others sitting behind her held their paddles on alternating sides of the canoe. It was so nearly perfect that Josh felt a sudden surge of pride.

"Hoe!"* Roger commanded. The paddles struck the smooth canal waters as one.

The canoe seemed to come alive, leaping ahead lightly. Every paddle staying in perfect rhythm, the crew members stroked together.

Josh didn't count the twelve strokes on a side, but when he heard Manuel's command of "hut!" on the thirteenth stroke, Josh realized that the pace was not going to be the easy forty-eight strokes a minute. He was picking up the pace.

Josh felt a strange stirring of excitement as the girls' paddles came out of the water as cleanly and quickly as the boys. "Hoe!" Manuel's clear order rang out.

The paddlers plunged their blades into the water on the opposite side of the canoe from where each had been stroking.

Even the steersman, Roger, was adding to the strokes as he could, although his main job was to steer the canoe. He called out, "Give a little extra now!"

Josh realized that Roger was following Tiffany's suggestion to show off in front of Kong. Josh's excitement bubbled up inside him. He lowered the video camera to his side and yelled, "Go, Tiffany and Marsha! Go for it! Power ten!"

Josh hoisted the video camera again and began shooting as Roger echoed, "Power ten!"

This command was usually given when passing another canoe or when the steersman saw the craft was in trouble from high waves or other danger. Now it was a simple practice with a purpose. They had to pass up Kong.

The canoe seemed to become a living thing. The fiberglass craft, like the ancient Hawaiian outriggers, swept majestically ahead. Through the viewfinder on the camera, Josh saw the surprised look on Kong's face.

Kong missed a stroke and his mouth dropped open as

the girls and boys swept even with his craft. They quickly passed. Josh wanted to yell with excitement, but he kept shooting footage until he heard Manuel's command.

"Wind off!" That meant to unwind, or stop paddling. All six boys in Kong's canoe had also slowed down.

"Maybe," Josh said aloud to himself, "just maybe we really can beat Kong, and the girls can race, too."

Then doubts arose when Kong turned and saw Josh on the canal bank. "Hey, you! Haole* boy. Scrimmage with Kong tomorrow."

Kong was challenging them to a practice race. Josh started to say no, but then thought better of it. Maybe that was a way to see how the actual race would go. Besides, he could videotape the scrimmage and they could check out the strengths and weaknesses of both teams.

"I'll ask the others when they get back," Josh called to Kong.

"Noon tomorrow," Kong replied as though that was the end of the discussion.

When Josh's sister and the other canoe racers returned to the shore, Josh told them about Kong's challenge. They accepted happily, anxious to find out more about their chances of actually beating Kong in the upcoming race.

On their way home, Josh said to his sister and Marsha, "Hey, you two did all right."

"Thanks!" the girls replied together as they went into the apartment.

When Josh opened the front door, Grandma Ladd

looked up from the occasional chair where she had been reading. Newspapers and books were stacked on both sides of her.

She said, "Joshua, I've been researching outrigger canoe racing. Did you know that the season runs from the fourth of June to the fifteenth of August? It's called the *summer regatta.*"

"That season is over," Josh reminded her. "Ours is a private race."

Grandma nodded. "I understand. But did you know that one year, in the women's forty-one-mile race from Molokai to Oahu, sudden squalls sprang up? Several canoes were swamped."

Josh shrugged. "Roger and Manuel say the canoes often become swamped, but it's no big deal. In a squall, everyone keeps paddling except Seats Four and Five. They bail the water out with buckets. We're going to practice that next week when we go out into the ocean for the first time. Shawn's father has rented a powerboat to go along with us."

"Good!" Grandma Ladd said. "I'll ride along and watch all of you practice."

"Maybe tomorrow you'd like to come see us scrimmage against Kong."

"I'll be there to cheer you on!"

Just then Nathan came in the room and asked, "Grandma, what's a squall?"

Grandma answered, "A squall is a sudden, violent

wind accompanied by rain, snow or sleet. But here in Hawaii that would only be rain, of course. The nice man at the weather bureau told me that local squalls can last for several minutes. Sometimes a waterspout unexpectedly comes along, too."

"What's that?" Nathan asked.

"It's like a tornado, except it's over water," Grandma explained. "You've heard about tornadoes on television. They're those violent winds that look like funnel-shaped clouds. Tornadoes wreck houses and anything else in their path. They happen mostly in the Midwest; you never see one in California. The weatherman told me that waterspouts sometimes come ashore in Hawaii. Then they're called a waterspout-tornado."

Josh remarked, "Roger or Manuel never mentioned anything like that."

"I guess that's because they don't come along too often," Grandma replied, picking up her knitting needles. "The weather-bureau man told me that you can see the waterspouts coming when you're out in the ocean, and you can usually escape them. I wouldn't worry about it."

"Yeah," Nathan said, looking up at his brother, "you got enough things to worry about. Like what's going to happen when King Kong beats you guys in the race."

Josh tried not to act annoyed with Nathan. "Kong's not going to beat us!"

"Now, Nathan, stop pestering your brother," Grandma said gently. "Let Joshua concentrate on winning the canoe race."

"Thanks, Grandma," Josh said. "Well, I'm going to take a shower."

As he turned around, the phone rang. He was only a step from it, so he picked it up. "Ladd family residence."

"Hello kid! Remember me?"

Josh recognized Rick's voice. "Yes."

"Good! I had to fly to the mainland on some business, but I'm back. And I want my package—now!"

Chapter Ten

OUT INTO THE OPEN SEA

Josh swallowed hard and glanced at his grandmother and brother. They both tensed, seeing something in Josh's face that made them concerned.

The man's voice on the phone asked, "You hear me?"

"I. . .I hear you."

"Okay, here's what you do. Bring the package to the boat house on Ala Wai Canal* right away. Just stand by the street and watch for me. I'll drive by and honk. You run over to the car and hand me the package. Understand?"

"Yes, but—"

"Come alone and don't be late!" The phone went dead.

Josh replaced the receiver and said with an edge of fear in his voice, "That was Rick. He wants me to bring the package to the boat house right away."

Nathan exclaimed, "Oh, oh! Now you're in for it."

"Nathan," Grandma Ladd said firmly, "I don't want to hear another word out of you!" She turned to Josh. "It'll be okay. I'll call the police and—"

"No, please, Grandma! If Rick sees them, he won't stop. But he'll be mad at me. I'll just meet him and say the big guy stole the package."

"You'd better talk to your father before you do anything."

Sighing, Josh agreed, "Okay, Grandma." He called the tourist publication that his father owned. The receptionist said John Ladd was with a client somewhere on the windward side of the island and couldn't be reached.

Josh hung up and explained that his father wasn't at work. Josh concluded, "I'll meet with this Rick and tell him what happened. He'll understand."

Nathan whispered, "Bet he won't."

Grandma said, "I'm calling Sergeant Tomashima. I won't risk having that man harm you because you showed up without his package."

A half hour later, Josh stood nervously by a light pole near the boat house. He scanned Ala Wai Boulevard. Traffic was normal. No police cars were in sight. Yet Grandma Ladd had called Sergeant Tomashima. He or Officer York must be somewhere out of sight, watching. Josh felt anxious, wishing he could have reached his father or at least had Tank come along.

Time passed slowly. Josh's mouth was dry. A silent prayer was on his lips. He stared down the street, searching for the old, green car, but none came.

It began to grow dark, and Josh was debating what to do. Even though his grandmother would have explained to John Ladd where Josh was, the boy was scared. Should he wait any longer?

The sound of a station wagon slowing made Josh look up. It was his father and grandmother. When his father got out of the vehicle, Josh protested, "Dad, you shouldn't have come!"

"That Rick fellow didn't show up, did he, Son?"

"No, but—"

"You've waited long enough," his father interrupted. "Get in. We're going home."

Josh took a slow, deep breath and looked around, but he didn't see Rick. "Okay, Dad." Josh opened the rear door and slid into the seat.

Later that evening when Josh was about ready for bed, he heard Kong calling from the parking lot. Josh went downstairs and across to the be-still tree.* He already knew why Kong wanted him.

"Got message, haole* boy! Rick planty* huhu* wit' you! He say, 'I see da kine* police wait. Next time, you do what I tell you, or too bad foh you.' Dah message. You unnerstand?"

"Yes."

"Good!" Kong leaned closer and asked softly, "Why he huhu wit' you?"

"I...I can't tell you." Josh turned and headed back across the lighted parking lot.

"Kong beat you in dah scrimmage come noontime. Maybe so I punch you out later foh not telling Kong when he ask!"

Josh groaned to himself, "How did I ever get into this mess?"

At noon the next day, the two crews met and quickly agreed on the scrimmage rules. The race would be from bridge to bridge along the Ala Wai Canal and back to the boat house. The three-mile round-trip would take about fifteen minutes.

Tiffany and Marsha wanted to be among the paddlers, but they reluctantly agreed to stay behind with Josh, Nathan and Grandma. Shawn limped over to take Seat One. Manuel sat behind him, followed by Big and Little K, then Tank, with Roger as steersman. Josh stood on the canal bank, the video camera perched on his right shoulder.

Both crews agreed Grandma Ladd could start off the race. She watched as both steersman called, "Reach out!"

When paddles from both canoes were poised, ready to strike the water, Grandma called out, "I've never done this before but here goes. One for the money. Two for the show. Three to make ready, and four to—Go!"

Josh watched the two canoes through the video camera's viewfinder. Josh heard the cassette begin to roll inside the camera; he felt the excitement rise to his throat.

He heard the commands from both steersmen, "Hoe!"* The paddles all hit at once, and the canoes shot ahead.

Tiffany, Nathan and Marsha started shouting encouragement and jumping up and down on the canal bank. Even Grandma was yelling, "Go! Go! Go!"

Josh got so excited he wanted to join in the shouting, but he forced himself to keep his mind on shooting the footage. He let out a groan as Kong's canoe pulled steadily ahead. Shawn's paddlers were straining mightily but falling behind rapidly.

Tiffany and Marsha's loud cries softened and died out. Josh could almost feel the crew members' enthusiasm draining away as Kong's canoe lengthened the distance ahead of them.

Josh was about to stop shooting when Kong's crew stopped paddling. Through the viewfinder, Josh saw the six boys turn and watch Shawn and his crew struggling to catch up.

"What's he doing?" Josh asked, still shooting.

"I don't know, Joshua," his grandmother said, "but I have a feeling. Yes, there they go again!"

As the trailing canoe started to come even with Kong's, Tiffany, Marsha and Nathan shouted encouragement through their cupped hands. Then Josh saw Kong's crew reach out with their paddles. They were too far away for Josh to hear the command, but he saw when they hit the water. Their canoe rapidly pulled away from Shawn's. Faint mocking laughter from Kong's outrigger drifted back to Josh.

He ground his teeth in frustration, but he kept shooting until both canoes were so far down the canal they appeared as bare spots in the viewfinder. Josh turned off the camera. The girls and Nathan had fallen silent as Kong's second spurt demonstrated how much faster his canoe and crew were.

Grandma said happily, "Maybe our team will catch Kong's canoe on the way back."

They waited in silence until Nathan pointed. "Here they come again! And look, Shawn's gaining!"

Everyone strained to see which of the two distant specks was ahead. Josh lifted the camera as Tiffany, Marsha, Grandma and Nathan began cheering lustily again.

Through the viewfinder, Josh could see that Shawn's outrigger was definitely gaining. Kong's crew kept paddling, but the second canoe slowly overtook it. That wonderful sight set Tiffany and Marsha into a frenzy; they jumped up and down, cheering.

"We're going to win!" Tiffany screeched in Josh's ear. "We're even with them. We're passing! Oh, no!"

Through the viewfinder, Josh saw it happen again. Shawn's canoe had pulled slightly ahead of Kong's. Then Kong's outrigger suddenly shot ahead. It pulled rapidly away. Kong and his crew crossed the finish line with loud, triumphant laughter. Josh turned off the camera.

Nathan protested, "That was mean! Kong was teasing them. He beat them twice. And he's still laughing."

Tiffany and Marsha continued grumbling while Grandma tried to remain cheerful. "This is only a practice.

We'll win in the big race."

Josh didn't say anything. He stood frowning as Kong's crew stepped ashore and continued their loud, boisterous celebration.

Hmm, he thought to himself. *Maybe I've just found Kong's weakness that Manuel was talking about.*

After dark, all of Josh's crew gathered around the video recorder to see the day's footage. They watched in gloomy silence as Kong's canoe took the lead, slowed tauntingly, and then swept ahead again. On the return trip, Kong did it again only to flash ahead to victory.

No one spoke when Josh got up to rewind the cassette. Roger's spirits were so low he said, "I didn't dream it would be this bad. Kong was so sure of winning that he showed off, let us catch up, and then rubbed our faces in the mud."

"Yeah," Tank said sadly, "we don't have a chance in the real race."

Josh turned around and faced everyone. "Hey! Don't give up! We've still got time."

"Oh, sure," Tank muttered. "Time to think about the terrible things that are going to happen when Kong wins the race and we have to be his servants."

Josh turned to Manuel. "I think maybe we've just seen the weakness you said Kong should have."

Manuel shook his head in disagreement. "That was no weakness. He played with us twice and then beat us."

Everyone started talking at once.

Josh raised his voice so all could hear him. "That's just it. He likes to show off, and maybe that's how we can beat him!"

A chorus of disagreement arose from the boys.

Josh said, "You're all missing the point. Look! I'm going to put the tape on fast forward and stop it at a couple of places. Then maybe you can see it for yourselves."

Everyone leaned forward to watch closely when Josh put the tape on pause. "See?" he said excitedly, walking over to touch the television screen. "Kong just showed us a possible way to beat him. Showing off is his weakness."

Not everyone was convinced, but the crew's spirits began to pick up.

Tiffany confessed, "I always hate to admit my younger brother may be right, but in this case, I think he is. And I'm glad!"

"Thanks, Tif," Josh said. "Now, let's all get prepared for next week when we start practicing on the open sea."

* * *

Josh watched Shawn as he limped around the canoe and the powerboat that Shawn's father had rented for them to use. Josh asked, "Shawn, why doesn't your father or mother ever come to see you practice?"

"They're both busy. Dad's a lawyer, and Mom's buying a boutique." Shawn's voice was slightly defensive. "But they give me anything I want." He waved toward the sleek, white powerboat and the outrigger canoe. "Besides, they're going to try to come to the big race."

Josh nodded but said nothing. He turned away, thinking, *They give him everything but themselves.*

Josh's father, mother, sister, brother and grandmother gathered on the beach near the powerboat and outrigger canoe rocking on the water.

Manuel raised his voice. "I've already explained how to paddle in the open sea, but let's review. Then we'll make some practice runs beyond the reef. After that, we'll change paddlers so Josh, Tiffany and Marsha can get some experience, too. For now, they'll ride in the Boston Whaler with Mr. Ladd and the others.

"As you know, it rains all year around here, with less rain in the summer. There's also less surf in the summer, but this time of the year the swells can sometimes be twenty-feet high. Two- to four-foot swells are normal; however, six- to eight-foot swells are dangerous. Swells may break into waves at six feet, but at twelve feet, you'll have breaking waves even in the ocean."

Josh gulped a little, picturing in his mind a rugged sea like that.

Manuel continued, "So we've got a lot to learn, including what happens if a wave comes over you from behind, which is called a *following wave.* The wave picks up the rear of the canoe and rapidly pushes it forward. Then we'll practice what to do when we're approaching a big wave. If you hit it wrong, the canoe will swamp. Josh will get video shots of us so we can study them later.

"Finally, in case we do swamp, we'll also practice jumping overboard into the ocean while two bail out the water. Then the rest of us will get back in the canoe and continue paddling. Okay, let's get started."

Josh's father was experienced in driving powerboats, so he took the wheel of the Boston Whaler. He had his mother and the three children put on life jackets, but the canoe racers didn't wear any. They only wore shorts, T-shirts to protect their backs from the sun, and baseball caps.

Mr. Ladd followed the outrigger as it pulled away from the shore. Josh watched several Windsurfers skimming along like colorful butterflies. He lifted the video camera and started to get some footage. Suddenly, he tensed as a man on a Windsurfer's rig veered away from the others and came straight toward the Boston Whaler.

That looks like Rick! Josh thought.

Chapter Eleven

A FINAL WARNING

For a moment, Josh watched with rising concern as Rick, riding the Windsurfer, headed straight for the Boston Whaler. Just as the boy started to call his father, another sailor suddenly cut in front of Rick. Josh heard a faint, angry shout as Rick took a sharp turn and fell into the ocean. Josh watched with relief as Rick swam toward his floating Windsurfer's rig. By the time he climbed back onto it, there would be no way he could catch up with the powerboat.

Josh took a deep breath and slowly let it out, thinking, *He'll try again. Sooner or later, he's going to catch up with me. What'll he do when he finds out I don't have his package?*

The thought was so scary that Josh didn't enjoy the canoe practice. He shot video footage, while everyone else in the powerboat shouted with excitement as the crew members practiced various maneuvers. Josh was thoughtfully silent.

Even that night, when everyone gathered around to

watch the video playback, Josh was so preoccupied with his relentless pursuer that he couldn't enjoy the footage.

Everyone laughed and shouted as the screen showed the crew practicing what to do in case of a squall. They all kept paddling, except Little K and Tank. They used cutoff plastic bleach bottles to bail water.

Josh's mother noticed her son's quietness. "What's the matter?" she asked.

Josh hesitated, then explained. "I saw Rick on a Windsurfer's rig, starting to follow us today."

"Did you tell your father?"

"No. I was going to, but nothing really happened."

His mother said softly, "I guess that Rick fellow is going to keep trying until he gets his package back. But I just can't imagine anyone being so foolhardy as to try taking something from you when your father was with you in the speedboat. Besides, why would Rick think you would have the package with you out in the ocean? I think he's just trying to scare you."

"He's doing a good job of it," Josh replied. "I'll talk to Dad when everyone's gone tonight."

After the apartment was quiet, Josh sat on the lanai* with his parents. He told his father about seeing Rick during practice. John Ladd listened thoughtfully, then went inside the apartment and called the police.

When he came back out on the small lanai, Mr. Ladd sighed. "They said there was no crime involved, so they can't do anything about it."

Mrs. Ladd protested, "They're scaring this family! Isn't that a crime?"

"Afraid not, since there's no direct threat. I guess we'll just have to wait. That fellow Rick will keep trying until this matter is resolved."

Days and nights went by with no further word from Josh's pursuer. The boy mechanically went about the canoe race practices and videotaping.

Why doesn't Rick call? he kept wondering.

The day before the great race, Josh awakened to the sound of distant thunder. "Oh, no," he groaned, rolling out of bed. "Bad weather! Just what we need for the race."

Later that morning, Kong called Josh to come outside. "Haole* boy," Kong said. "Rick say you bring dah package for shuh. He'll see you at dah race."

"I don't have the package," protested Josh.

"Rick be planty* huhu* wit' you. You bettah find dah package," Kong said as he walked away. He laughed and then shouted over his shoulder. "We beat you good."

By the time Josh got back up to the apartment his family was in such a hurry to leave, he didn't tell them about Kong's warning. When Josh's family arrived at the Honolulu Airport for the short flight to Maui, the sun was bright, and the sky was clear except for huge piles of white clouds hovering far out over the ocean.

"Those are cumulonimbus clouds,"* his father explained.

Grandma remarked, "They're beautiful, like great

mounds of whipped cream!"

Her son chuckled. "Actually, they're a class of clouds that suggest thunderstorm conditions."

Grandma asked, "You mean it's going to storm?"

"No," John Ladd shook his head. "Those clouds have passed us and are well out to sea. They'll be gone before the race tomorrow, unless the wind changes directions, but I doubt that it will."

A rental car was waiting at the Maui airport for the Ladd family to drive down to Maalaea Bay,* where everyone assembled at the launch site.

Shawn's parents didn't show up, but Mr. Tremaine had arranged for another outrigger and a powerboat for their use. The crew members took the canoe out for a late afternoon practice. Mr. Ladd followed in the Boston Whaler, but he had to turn back.

"Motor's not running quite right," he told the man at the boat rental agency. "Would you please check it over? I don't want any problems tomorrow when I follow these young canoe enthusiasts to Molokini* and back."

Later that day, Shawn's crew watched Kong's crew use inflatable rollers to ease their outrigger into the bay. "Hey, haole boy!" Kong called, waving his paddle, "You want to give up now?"

Josh wanted to lash back in anger, but he managed to keep his voice calm. "It's the end of a race that counts," he said, quoting a saying he had heard his father often use.

After practice, Josh walked back to the condominium

overlooking the bay. For the night before the race, they had rented two places, one for Josh's family and the other for the rest of the crew members. Tank's sister, Marsha, was staying with the Ladd family so she could be with Tiffany.

At sundown, Josh watched Shawn limping along the beach. *I wonder,* Josh asked himself, *how he feels when his parents are always too busy to be there for him?*

That night everyone gathered around the TV for one final review of all the videocassettes Josh had shot of both Shawn's crew and Kong's various practices. It also included footage taken that afternoon when Mr. Ladd had turned back with the faulty powerboat.

"What do you think?" Grandma Ladd asked, her knitting needles clicking furiously as always. "All of you want to win this race. So you will—right?"

The boys let out a cheerful chorus, "Yes!"

Shawn stood and took a limping step forward. Standing in front of the television screen, he raised his hand to quiet everyone. "I've got to say something."

Everyone fell silent while Shawn spoke. "Winning this race tomorrow will give me a chance to prove I'm equal to anyone with two good legs, including Kong. Besides, my father told me before I left Honolulu that if I win...."

Josh was surprised that Shawn's voice broke suddenly. He tightly pressed his lips together. Josh glimpsed a brightness in Shawn's eyes.

Shawn gained control of his voice and continued. "My

father says that if we win he'll take me to California for a whole week. My dad's never taken me on a vacation before."

While everyone else exclaimed happily for Shawn, Josh was silent. He realized for the first time that Shawn wasn't trying to prove he was everyone else's equal; he was trying to prove it to his father.

"Shawn," Josh said huskily, "we're going to do it."

Shawn started to say something, then suddenly turned his head away and hurried outside into the night.

Josh stared thoughtfully after him for a moment then turned back to face the others as they walked toward the door. He clapped his hand hard on Manuel's shoulders. "We're going to do it, Manuel!"

"Sure are!" Manuel agreed.

"We're going to win!" Josh said the same thing with the same fierce intensity to Roger, Tank and Big and Little K as each went out the door.

Each one nodded emphatically. When the door was closed, Josh turned to look at his family. Doubts flooded the boy's mind. It was one thing to say it; to actually win the race was an entirely different thing.

Grandma Ladd laid down her knitting needles and walked over to her grandson. "Joshua, I am proud to be part of your family," she said huskily.

When she picked up her knitting and hurried down the hall to her bedroom, Josh looked thoughtfully at his father, mother, Marsha, Tiffany and Nathan.

Nathan said quietly, "Grandma's right, Josh."

Josh saw his parents nod just as the phone rang. Josh's heart skipped a beat as his father answered it. He listened, then his face hardened. His voice took on a crisp, authoritative tone. "Yes, he's here. Whom shall I say is calling?"

Mr. Ladd paused and then added, "I'm his father, but I will not put him on the line until you've answered my—"

Mr. Ladd replaced the receiver and told his family. "Whoever it was hung up."

"It had to be Rick!" Josh said with feeling.

"I'm sure you're right, Son. But how did he know you were here?"

Josh shrugged. "Kong told me to bring the package yesterday, but I told him I didn't have it."

While the family debated what to do, Josh heard Kong calling from outside the condominium. "Hey, you! Haole boy!"

Josh looked at his family. "That's Kong with a message from Rick!"

Josh's mother asked, "Josh, what will we do?"

"I could call the police," Mr. Ladd said, "but they'll say the same thing the officers in Honolulu said."

As Kong shouted again, Josh made up his mind. "I'll go find out for sure."

"I'll come with you, Son."

"No, Dad! Please! Kong might take it wrong if I came out with you. I'll be okay."

Kong was waiting by a rubber-tree plant. He didn't waste any time but promptly delivered his message. "Da kine* Rick, he planty huhu you now! Say you bring da kine package on canoe tomorrow! He come 'longside and take it wikiwiki!* You not do, him feed you to dah sharks!"

That night Josh didn't sleep well. He was so deep in thought about what to do that he wasn't aware the trade winds had died down. When he felt a strange silence and a heaviness in the still night air, he suddenly realized the wind had shifted.

"Kona,"* he muttered aloud to himself. "South wind. Yeah, I hear the thunder." He got up and walked to the window just as lightning split the sky. *Maybe there won't be a race tomorrow. Or maybe it'll be like today and blow over by race time.*

Early the next morning, the sky was polished clean of any storm signs, except for the dense, towering clouds over the ocean. Somehow they seemed closer than the day before. But Josh couldn't think about the weather. He had to get ready for the race. Everyone ate breakfast and hurried to the launch site. Final preparations were made for the great canoe race.

At 8:45 a.m., both outriggers were in the water, and the crews were eager to be off. Josh's father seemed satisfied with the adjustments that had been made on the powerboat.

Josh asked, "Kong, where's your powerboat?"

The big kid smiled. "Kong don't need no stinkin' 'nother boat! Jus' da kine canoe." He tapped the outrigger with a powerful hand. "You malihinis* ready to lose dah race?"

Josh didn't answer but turned away with concern. He didn't like the idea of even someone like Kong taking a risk on the open sea without a back-up boat.

Josh's thoughts were interrupted by his father. He was calling for all of their team to come together near the outrigger. Mr. Ladd said, "Shawn, I don't know how you feel about such things, but ours is a praying family. I know that Roger is a Buddhist,* but he said he wouldn't mind if I ask for everyone's safety in this race."

Shawn shrugged. "My folks just work; they don't hold much with religion, but I guess we could all use a little prayer now and then."

Mr. Ladd nodded. "Fine. Then I'll ask God's blessing and protection for everyone."

Josh automatically bowed his head as his father began to pray. But Josh didn't close his eyes. He stole a glance at Kong and his crew. They were standing by their canoe, watching the tight little circle around John Ladd.

Kong laughed, throwing back his big head. "Da kine malihinis goin' need planty moh dan pray to beat Kong!" he said loudly enough for Josh to hear. " 'Specially when Rick shows up!"

The laughter of Kong and his crew members still echoed in Josh's ears as everyone took his place in the canoes. The air was tense with excitement.

Josh glanced over at Kong, sitting triumphantly in the first position in the adjacent outrigger. Josh studied the other five boys seated single file behind Kong. They were as big as men, with powerful arms and shoulders. They were all jeering and taunting Shawn and his crew.

Shawn's canoe was ready. Josh wanted to be where Tank sat in the Five Seat, but it had been decided Josh would ride in the Boston Whaler with Tiffany and Marsha, their relief paddlers. Shawn was poised at the bow, followed by Manuel, Big and Little K and Tank with Roger in the stern.

Josh lifted the video camera to his shoulder and focused, automatically framing the crew in the outrigger with the towering white clouds in the distance.

Grandma again acted as starter. "Ready!" she called.

"Reach out!" Roger's command was almost one with Kong's steersman.

"Set!" Grandma cried.

Josh felt his blood speed up as the six boys in each canoe moved their paddles in perfect harmony over the bay's water.

"Go!" Grandma yelled.

"Hoe!"* The cry sounded together from both outriggers. Every paddle hit the water and the canoes shot forward. The race was on!

Chapter Twelve

ATTACK OF THE WINDSURFER

Tiffany and Marsha climbed into the powerboat. Josh sat behind them, settling down with his video camera. As his father pulled away from the dock, Josh looked back to see his little brother, mother and grandmother waving from the shore.

They planned to cheer Shawn's crew on to victory when the race ended. Still, Josh knew it was going to take something special for Shawn's crew to beat the experienced Kong and his paddlers.

The two outrigger canoes looked as if they were still close together as they passed the McGregor Point Lighthouse, marking the end of Maalaea Bay.* Josh kept shooting video footage as the canoes entered the open sea.

Josh looked behind them. A number of Windsurfers zipped about like water bugs on a mill pond. Most hugged the shoreline. Only a few rigs sliced boldly across the open sea.

Josh started to shoot the powerboat's wake. He saw a Windsurfer's rig glide from behind the breakwater. For a second, Josh thought the sailor was Rick, but the bright red and yellow sail hid the sailor's face. The Windsurfer turned away. Josh breathed easier and turned to watch the race.

The Boston Whaler soon caught up with the two canoes. They still seemed about even as they headed for Molokini.* When the Ladd powerboat pulled even with the two outriggers, Tiffany cupped her hands and yelled, "Great going, guys! Kong hasn't gotten ahead of you, yet!"

"Yea!" Marsha yelled across the water. "You're beating Kong!"

Josh saw Kong's big head jerk when he heard the girls' taunting cheers. Josh could tell from the look on Kong's face that the girls' words had angered him. Josh shifted his video camera toward Kong's canoe just in time to see that he was right.

"Power ten!" The call from Kong's canoe was loud and clear. Instantly, Kong's paddlers increased their tempo. The canoe surged ahead, rapidly dropping Shawn's craft far behind.

Josh growled, "Why did you girls say that?"

Tiffany and Marsha didn't answer. Josh realized they were sorry for angering Kong and egging him on.

Josh lowered his camera as Kong's crew eased off and stopped well ahead of Shawn's craft.

"What's Kong doing?" Tiffany asked.

Josh answered, "He's showing off again. Maybe Kong's

overconfidence will foul him up. If only we get a chance to use it against him."

The powerboat sped some distance ahead of both canoes. Mr. Ladd throttled back but didn't turn off the motor. Josh watched Shawn's canoe head for the Boston Whaler; it was time for Josh and Tank to change places.

Well out to sea, near Molokini, Josh saw another outrigger just becoming visible. Josh guessed it held a crew of men out for a fun run. Josh also saw the same Windsurfer with the red and yellow sail. He must have circled out around them, and now he was ahead of them. Josh heard a helicopter overhead. He knew that choppers sometimes followed the Windsurfers to rescue the sailors if they became tired and couldn't get back to land.

Kong's canoe passed the Boston Whaler. His crew jeered and taunted Josh and the others with him. Josh ignored them while he waited for Shawn's canoe. When it came even with the Boston Whaler, Josh's father said, "Okay, Son, get ready to change places."

Josh carefully handed his video camera to Tiffany and pulled off his life jacket.

Tiffany asked, "What about Marsha and me?"

Josh answered, "We've got to round Molokini and start back. Then maybe you and Marsha can paddle."

"Maybe?" Tiffany flared. "Are you saying you guys are planning to keep Marsha and me from being in this race?"

Josh kicked off his sandals and slid over the side of

the powerboat into the ocean. "That's Shawn's decision," he said evasively.

His sister cried angrily, "If you cut us out, I hope you lose!"

Josh caught a warning look from his father. Josh didn't answer his sister, knowing their father disliked his children to squabble. Josh also knew his father was silently reminding him that the girls had practiced and had a right to become paddlers.

Josh, treading in the water, turned and watched Shawn's outrigger come along the right side of the Boston Whaler.

"Ready, Tank?" Josh yelled across the small expanse of sea that now separated the two vessels.

His friend nodded and slipped over the left side of the canoe into the water. It was a maneuver they had practiced many times because speed was essential in changing paddlers during the race.

Josh climbed in the canoe and quickly took his place. He picked up his paddle and grinned at the other boys who were watching him. "We're going to beat them!" Josh cried.

There were general murmurs of agreement, then Manuel called, "Reach out!"

Josh obeyed, feeling the excitement of the race sweep over him in a new way. It had been one thing to sit in a powerboat and watch; it was quite another to be in the race. Josh extended his paddle to the left in nearly perfect harmony with the other canoe racers. Molokini rose out of the ocean dead ahead. It was a kind of beacon marking the halfway spot of the race.

Josh was sitting barely eighteen inches above the water, which was getting rough. Out of the corner of his eye, he saw Tank sit down in the powerboat and slip on a life jacket. Mr. Ladd started to rev up the boat's motor, but it sputtered and died. Josh realized that repairs the night before had not been entirely satisfactory.

"Hoe!"* Manuel called.

Josh forgot about the Boston Whaler; he thrust his paddle into the water with the others. As he stroked the first time, the strain in his back and shoulder muscles felt good. He glanced ahead and saw Kong's canoe. *We're gaining on him,* Josh thought.

He was aware that Manuel had picked up the pace; it was closer to seventy strokes than the usual sixty in racing. The sensation of speed made Josh's blood flow faster, and he felt a joyful excitement. Josh saw that they had almost caught up with Kong. Both canoes were rapidly overtaking the third, lone outrigger.

That's when Josh saw something else—the guy on the Windsurfer with the red and yellow sail. The sailor suddenly swerved and zoomed straight for Josh's outrigger.

"Hey!" Josh cried. "It's Rick! Is he going to ram us?"

Rick swept in fast and silently. Josh was sure they were going to collide. All six boys in the outrigger broke their rhythm, and the craft slowed down. But at the last second, just a few feet away from the canoe, Rick cut sharply around and dropped the sail. The rig coasted to a stop in the choppy sea.

"Hey, kid! Hand over the package!"

"Rick!" Josh exclaimed. In the excitement of the race preparations, he had forgotten that he had been told to bring the mysterious package on the trip.

"I...I,..." Josh stuttered, watching the thin-faced man gliding beside the canoe, his left hand outstretched.

"No stalling!" Rick yelled, his face dark with sudden anger. "Hand it over right now or I'll—" He reached back quickly with his left hand and plucked a baseball bat from where it had been clipped to the mast.

Josh instinctively drew back and cried out, "I don't have it!"

"What? Kid, don't lie to me!"

"Honest, Mister! A big guy named Larry stole it."

"Larry?" Rick thundered in surprise. "I should have known!"

All of a sudden Josh realized that the helicopter sounded like it was closer to them. Josh looked up in time to see the aircraft hovering just overhead. A man's authoritative voice called over a loudspeaker. "This is the police! Jackson, drop your weapon. Right now!"

For the first time, Josh learned Rick's last name. The boy watched the side door of the helicopter slide open. Sergeant Tomashima braced himself there with a microphone in hand. Officer York and another armed policeman in uniform crouched in the doorway. Rick hesitated, then let the bat fall into the waves. At once the two officers began lowering a rope ladder.

Sergeant Tomashima's voice boomed again over the loudspeaker. "Grab hold of that ladder and climb up. Do it now!"

The thin-faced man reached up and grabbed the lowest rung of the dangling ladder and reluctantly started climbing. Moments later, the officers reached out and pulled Rick into the chopper. The side door slid shut. The aircraft climbed steeply upward.

"Wow!" Roger cried from behind Josh. "That was close!"

"Yeah," Josh agreed. "But I sure wish I knew what that was all about. How'd they know Rick was coming after me?"

"Doesn't matter now!" Manuel called. "We've got a race to win, and the water's getting rough. Reach out!"

Josh hadn't noticed that the ocean's waves had become so choppy. They had been moderate swells, but now he guessed the waves were running about four feet high. The clouds that had towered in the distant sky now seemed closer, too.

Rick's unexpected appearance and the police intervention had excited Josh. He was happy to have something physical to do to use up the excess energy that flooded every inch of his body. Apparently the same was true of the other five boys, for the outrigger leaped ahead on Manuel's command.

Josh's eyes lifted again to see where Kong's canoe was. It had slowed and stopped some distance ahead. All of Kong's crew members had apparently been watching the Windsurfer and the unexpected appearance of the police helicopter.

"We're gaining on Kong," Manuel called. "If he keeps stopping or slowing up to show off, we can still beat him."

"That's his weakness—overconfidence," Josh whispered fiercely. "If there were just some way to make him stop long enough."

Josh looked toward Molokini, trying to gauge how close they were. He wondered where the lone third canoe had disappeared. He had seen it just before Rick's unexpected appearance. But now the outrigger was nowhere in sight. Farther out, where he thought he'd seen the canoe, the waves looked as though they were higher and rougher.

"Maybe that third canoe is down in one of those troughs," Josh muttered aloud to himself, "and it'll come up on a crest in a moment."

It did, but not the way Josh had expected. The canoe was swamped. The crew had jumped out of the canoe, so they wouldn't weigh the swamped craft down. Four men were bailing with their hands or with plastic containers. A fifth crewman was easing back into the canoe from the left side.

Only one member wasn't helping. His right arm flopped uselessly in the water. His face rested wearily against the pontoon; the man was seriously hurt. Without a life jacket, he seemed to be slipping slowly into the ocean; his grip was weakening.

Shawn called from the One Seat, "Those guys are in big trouble!"

From his seat directly in front of Josh, Little K yelled, "Kong's close enough to stop and help!"

Josh watched hopefully as Kong's canoe drew even with the hapless victims. They were yelling and waving their hands.

"Kong's not going to stop!" Josh exclaimed. "He's going right on by. We have to help them."

Big K asked, "You mean, let Kong win?"

Josh exclaimed, "We can't just go on and leave them!"

Big K said, "No, but there goes the race. And all that it means to every one of us!"

Shawn called over his shoulder. "It doesn't matter. Let's go help those guys before the injured man drowns."

As Shawn's crew obeyed, Josh heard taunting laughter from Kong's canoe. It swept on toward Molokini and almost certain victory.

Chapter Thirteen

TERROR AT SEA

As Shawn's canoe eased up alongside the swamped outrigger, Josh saw that all six crewmen were in their twenties. Two were bailing with plastic buckets. One was using an old bleach bottle with the top cut off. Two other crewmen seemed to be helping the sixth man, who clung weakly to the pontoon.

One of the stranded men called out to Shawn's crew, "Thanks for stopping! A following wave swamped us."

He pointed to the nearly unconscious man in the water. "Matt broke his arm. And Pete cut his leg; it's bleeding pretty bad. We have to get them out of the water—fast!" He glanced around nervously.

Josh knew they were thinking the same thing. Shark attacks were rare, but the great fish were out in the ocean. If the sharks followed the scent of blood, they might attack the helpless men. But if the six men tried to find safety in Shawn's already-loaded canoe, would any of them survive?

Josh looked at Shawn for a decision since he was the

leader. Shawn half hoisted himself from his seat in the bow, shifting his crippled left leg. "Let's get the injured on board first. Then we'll see what we can do about the rest of your crew."

The man who acted as leader called, "Thanks! We'll be okay once we bail out our canoe."

Josh leaned over the left side where the pontoon gave greater stability. He reached out with the Lama brothers to grasp the semiconscious man being lifted and pushed by the men in the water. It was tricky and risky, but soon both the man with the broken arm and the one with the long leg-slash had been eased over the side into the canoe.

Josh was tempted to cry out a warning as the overloaded canoe began to sink under the extra weight. Instead, he whispered a silent prayer and joined Roger and Little K in giving first aid to the injured men.

From the water, their leader said, "While the rest of us finish bailing out our canoe, we'd be mighty grateful if you boys could wait until we're safely on board again."

Shawn nodded. "Okay," he said, "but please make it fast!"

"Thanks," the blond man replied. "You boys are really all right!"

Shawn twisted around in the canoe's bow so he could look directly at the five boys sitting single file behind him. "We'd better decide on what to do if they don't succeed in saving their outrigger. Should we take these two injured men back to shore and forget the race?"

Manuel reminded Shawn, "It's your canoe, so it should be your choice."

Josh knew how much it meant to all of them to finish the race and win if possible. He turned to scan the rising waves. They were now high enough so that small whitecaps were starting to break. A fine, salt spray hit the boy's face and stung his eyes.

"I say, we've got to take them back," Shawn said.

Slowly, the four boys in front of Josh nodded. He turned to look at Roger.

"Maybe that's not necessary!" he said, turning to point behind them. "Look! Here comes your father, Josh!"

"You're right! It's my dad!"

In moments, John Ladd eased the powerboat closer. Josh called through cupped hands, "Dad, two of the men are hurt bad!"

Mr. Ladd replied, "I don't dare turn off this motor, or it may never start again. I'll ease in as close as I can; then we'll take the injured aboard."

John Ladd turned to the girls. "Tiffany, you and Marsha grab a couple of life jackets. Throw them over to Josh and the other boys. Son, help those injured men into the jackets."

The orders continued nonstop as Mr. Ladd looked toward the swamped canoe. "You men, divide up! Two of you swim over to the boys' canoe and help move those injured ones.

"The last couple of you swim over here and climb

aboard. Be ready to help the girls get the injured aboard. I've got to keep this vessel pointed into the waves so we won't get hit broadside and tip over."

Everyone worked furiously while the waves got higher and rougher. They threatened to smash the idling power-boat into one or both of the big outriggers.

But at last the two injured men were aboard the Boston Whaler. A third man decided to ride along to help care for the men who had been hurt. The other three men chose to save their canoe by continuing to bail it out. Then they would return to shore.

When it was over, Josh collapsed on Five Seat with a deep sigh of relief.

His father called, "You boys had better turn around and follow me back. I don't like the looks of this weather!"

Josh shot a quick look at the horizon. The great masses of clouds rose in threatening columns. Josh knew by their shape that strong winds were coming with those clouds. Still, they seemed a long way off.

Shawn said, "Excuse me, Mr. Ladd, but we can't do that!"

"Shawn," Mr. Ladd called across from the powerboat, "the last I saw of Kong, he was far ahead of you boys. It may be impossible to beat him now."

"Mr. Ladd, Sir, we may not win, but we're going to finish!"

As the boys' canoe rose to the crest of a monstrous wave, Josh caught a flash of sunlight on a distant paddle.

Before the outrigger slid back down into a trough, Josh recognized whose it was.

He cupped his hands and called, "Dad, Kong stopped up ahead! He must have waited to watch the rescue. We're going to finish, and maybe we can still beat Kong!"

Mr. Ladd hesitated, then nodded. "I'll run these people to shore, change boats and be right back! I should catch up with you boys on the other side of Molokini* and follow you in!"

Tiffany yelled, "When we get back, you guys had better let Marsha and me paddle!"

Mr. Ladd revved up the Boston Whaler's motor and headed back toward Maalaea Bay.* The swamped outrigger was soon bailed out enough; the three remaining men assured the boys they could make it back to shore.

Manuel prepared to get the boys' outrigger back into action. "Listen up! We've got to make up for lost time! Reach out!"

The seas were running dangerously high by the time the boys rounded Molokini's crescent-shaped islet and headed down the other side. The wind seemed to have shifted. The clouds, which had been on the distant horizon, were now moving rapidly toward the boys' canoe.

It's going to rain, Josh thought. *I just hope it holds off until this race is over.*

The boys' outrigger fairly surged through the water as if anxious to beat the bad weather. The six boys stroked their paddles in the water, moving in perfect harmony.

Josh searched the horizon ahead, but he didn't see any sign of Kong's canoe. Maui was visible straight ahead now. The sight of land ahead and the bad weather closing in on them made Josh paddle harder.

Shawn called over his shoulder, "Look what's coming off to our left! Josh, there's your father's boat."

Josh agreed, "It is my dad. But I thought he was going to change boats."

Roger said from behind Josh, "Maybe he couldn't do that on short notice. Anyway, this one seems to be running all right now."

In a few minutes, Mr. Ladd throttled back and slowed at a safe distance from the outrigger. Tank, Tiffany and Marsha were still with him. Mr. Ladd called, "Everybody okay?"

"We're all okay," Shawn yelled back.

Tiffany started pulling off her life jacket. "Then it's Marsha's and my turn to paddle."

Josh shook his head. *Girls!* he thought. *We're behind in the race, and they want to paddle!*

"Yeah," Marsha agreed, stripping off her life jacket. "You guys promised."

"No, we didn't!" Josh yelled. "Besides, this is no time to change paddlers. We've got to catch Kong."

Mr. Ladd said above the idling motor, "Excuse me, boys, but you did let the girls train with the hopes they could be relief paddlers. But whatever you do, I'd suggest you get at it. I don't like the way the sky's looking!"

Josh started to protest again, but Shawn said, "You girls deserve a chance to be in on the finish." He turned his head to look at the single file of boys behind him. "Okay with you guys?"

The boys didn't respond with enthusiasm, but they knew that their chances of winning were slim. Kong's canoe was still out of sight. Josh figured Shawn had decided that finishing was almost as honorable as winning.

Manuel gave the command to wind off, and the outrigger slowed down. It plunged and bucked in the waves, but Roger as steersman held the bow into the oncoming waves. Big and Little K offered to give up their seats, so they slid over the canoe's side into the ocean. They clung to the left side of the outrigger while the girls eased aboard beside them. When Tiffany and Marsha were seated, the brothers took a few powerful swimming strokes and slid into the powerboat.

Mr. Ladd eased the Boston Whaler away to a safe distance and Manuel gave the command, "Reach out!"

Manuel set a brisk pace. The canoe sliced through the choppy water. Josh eagerly scanned the rolling seas ahead, hoping for a glimpse of Kong's canoe. He saw nothing. *Has he pulled that far ahead?* Josh wondered.

Mr. Ladd revved the motor on the Boston Whaler and ran close alongside the canoe. Big and Little K shouted and pointed to something behind the paddlers.

Josh turned his head with the others in the canoe.

"Squall coming!" Big K yelled. "We can outrun it in

this boat, but you're going to get wet!"

Shawn and his crew had practiced for all kinds of possible emergencies, including squalls. Josh tried to remember what he had learned.

Thoughts about squalls flashed in his mind like strobe lights: *A sudden, violent wind up to twenty-five miles an hour, accompanied by rain. Clouds dark but usually not black. Waves can run five to eight feet high. They break up in the wind, making whitecaps. Squalls last ten to fifteen minutes. Visibility isn't bad, maybe a mile, but up to an inch and a quarter of rain may fall in an hour. Squalls can swamp outriggers!*

Manuel raised his voice. "It looks as if the squall will brush by us. We won't get caught in the middle of it. Let's paddle hard and try to outrun it. But if it does hit, you know what to do."

Josh paddled with every muscle in his body, his eyes watching the storm front. It was so wide that it quickly stretched beyond the canoe toward shore. *Kong is going to be caught in it for sure!* Josh thought.

The squall seemed to be running alongside the canoe about a quarter-mile away. Josh watched in fascination. The clouds were dark but not black. There was some lightning and thunder. A light drizzle fell on the canoe racers.

Josh looked behind Roger, who was sitting in the stern. A massive cumulonimbus cloud* rose fearfully into the threatening sky. The towering column flickered with lightning.

Nobody else in the canoe looked around. They continued their furious, rhythmic paddling. Josh was too fascinated to take his eyes off the strange cloud.

As he watched, something like a giant thread dipped from the cloud. It twisted and curled downward near the ocean's surface, writhing erratically, like a giant, one-armed octopus.

It looked like a tornado or one of those freak twisters Josh had seen on television. But it wasn't black and threatening like a tornado.

Josh stared at the parent cloud that had spawned the strange, twisting column. He could almost see through the end of the long, writhing arm as it reached down toward the ocean. The strange formation was about a hundred yards across and had a hazy gray color, like rapidly swirling water.

"Hey, what's that?" he cried out.

The others turned around to see. Josh heard a sharp intake of breath from Roger. He yelled, "Waterspout! A tornado on water!"

Sudden fear seared through Josh as if he had been burned with hot oil. As he watched in fascinated terror, the end of the twisting arm touched the ocean.

Josh yelled, "It's coming straight for us!"

Chapter Fourteen

RACE FOR LIFE

For a moment, no one spoke. Everyone stared in fearful fascination at the waterspout. It extended from its glowering parent cloud in the sky almost down to the frothy ocean's surface. The gray mass, driven by fierce internal winds, twisted and turned erratically, moving toward the canoe. Now the spout resembled a gigantic elephant's trunk, swaying ponderously back and forth, seeking something to destroy.

The paddlers automatically stopped stroking, although Manuel had not given the command to wind off. As the outrigger lost speed, it slipped and plunged sideways down a monstrous wave into a deep trough.

Manuel's experience quickly came to his aid. "Reach out! Reach out!" His voice crackled with tension.

The crew obeyed instantly, their eyes riveted on the awesome hundred-yard-wide funnel of destruction twisting toward them.

"Hit!" Manuel shrieked.

Josh plunged his paddle into the angry, billowing waves

with great force. He threw all the strength of his back and shoulders into the stroke. He was only vaguely aware that Roger had gained control of the outrigger's direction. Under Roger's expert handling, the canoe's bow slowly came about to face into the oncoming waves, as a mountain of water crashed over the canoe.

Josh instinctively closed his eyes to protect them against the stinging salt spray. When he opened them again, the canoe was half-filled with water.

We're going to swamp! his mind screamed, but Roger's voice cut through Josh's fear.

"No time to bail! Everybody keep paddling. Power ten! Paddle like you never have before!"

Josh tore his gaze from the waterspout, which still chased them like a hound on a hot trail. *It's gaining on us!* he thought wildly.

He wanted to cry out with fear, but he couldn't even speak. He needed all his energy to paddle. He looked ahead of them to see how close the canoe was to land. He couldn't see the shore because a curtain of hard rain hung between the outrigger and safety.

Kong is in there somewhere, Josh thought. For a moment, he felt a strange sense of gladness. Kong, who had made Josh's life miserable for so long, was at the mercy of the squall.

His thoughts were interrupted by a sudden downpour. The sky was like a gigantic plastic bag filled with water. Suddenly the bottom blew out and dumped water all over them. The rain fell so hard Josh could barely see Shawn paddling in the bow. Kong's canoe was lost in the downpour and so was the Boston Whaler.

Strangely, it wasn't windy. The main body of the squall had not hit them. They might have a chance, unless the waterspout caught them. If that happened, the canoe would be destroyed instantly.

Josh heard a low, fervent prayer from in front of him. "Oh, Lord, help us!"

Through the sheets of rain, Josh saw Marsha seated directly in front of him. She was soaked. Her hair hung down like a wet mop, but her bare arms were still flashing in perfect rhythm with the other crew members.

In front of Marsha, Josh's older sister was also praying aloud. She was equally drenched, but her shoulders and arms moved in harmony with Manuel's calls.

Josh called out, "Tif, Marsha, are you okay?"

"Just...scared!" Marsha answered without turning around.

"Me, too!" Tiffany called back. Her voice was almost lost in the sound of driving rain.

"Keep paddling!" Josh urged. "We'll be okay!"

They paddled on, driven by desperation and the desire to live. Josh glanced behind them. The waterspout was now a huge frightening monster, moving faster and more erratically, sweeping closer to them.

Josh breathed heavily from paddling so hard. His muscles threatened to knot up in spasms. He prayed silently, fervently, his arms driving the paddle into the tossing waves with every ounce of his waning strength.

As suddenly as it began, the heavy downpour eased off. The rain drifted toward the horizon on their right. Only a light drizzle continued to fall.

"It missed us!" exclaimed Josh with relief. "The squall just brushed by us." He stole another quick look behind them. The waterspout was still kicking up spray on the ocean's surface, so they weren't out of danger yet.

He opened his mouth to report this to the others, but Shawn suddenly yelled, "Look up ahead! There's Kong. He's stopped right in our way. Roger, steer around him, fast!"

Roger obeyed instantly. Through the light rain that still fell, Josh saw the outrigger's bow swing sharply to the left. The craft slid toward Kong's canoe with enough clearance so they could pass safely.

Josh glanced around for his father's powerboat, but it was still nowhere in sight. *Maybe it's just hidden by the passing squall,* Josh thought. *Or maybe the motor quit on him.* He shook off the thought and looked at the distant screen of water.

As Shawn's outrigger passed closer to Kong's, Josh saw that Kong's crew had stopped paddling. The vessel rode deep in the water. The top side of the boat only had about a six-inch clearance. They were clearly in danger of swamping. And they had no Boston Whaler with a crew of boys to help.

Everyone was bailing. The boys in Seats Four and Five used their plastic pails. The other four boys scooped water out with their bare hands. It was obvious that they had nearly swamped, but they were making headway in emptying the outrigger's hull of excess water.

Josh started to shout a warning about the waterspout. He turned to point out the danger to the unsuspecting Kong and his crew.

But just as Josh was about to warn them, he stopped and stared in disbelief. He called, "It's gone! The waterspout's gone!"

Everyone in Shawn's outrigger broke out in cheers. Manuel gave the tired command, "Wind off!"

The exhausted paddlers gladly obeyed. Their canoe rolled heavily in the rough seas, but Roger kept the craft under control.

Josh wanted to jump up and down with relief, but that wasn't wise in a half-swamped outrigger. Obviously, the other crew members felt the same. To ease the tension of having just escaped a brush with death, they started to tease Kong and his crew.

Shawn cupped his hands and shouted, "Hey, Kong! Did you stop to admire the scenery?"

Roger laughed, "You want us to tow you in?"

Manuel yelled, "Maybe you stopped to gloat because you thought you were so far ahead we'd never catch you. Now we're going to win for sure!"

Kong stopped bailing and looked up. Barely fifty feet

away, the last of the light, misty rain passed and bright sunshine glowed down on the sea. Its bright rays bathed Kong's big body.

He tossed another cupped handful of water overboard. "Kong got you beat long time ago, so stop. Den da kine* squall snuck up on us!"

Shawn raised his voice. "Good thing the waterspout didn't get any of us!"

Kong's brown eyes opened wide. "Yeah, Bruddah!* We all be history!"

Josh, remembering the girls' prayers, said, "We had some help!"

Kong blinked, not understanding. Josh didn't try to explain.

He was still so excited from having escaped the waterspout's fury that he was bursting with energy in spite of his aching, tired muscles. He asked seriously, "Kong, are you going to make it to shore okay?"

Kong swelled his mighty chest and pounded on it with a massive fist. "You bet!" He started to say something else boastful but stopped suddenly and stared. It was obvious he was seeing water-soaked and disheveled Tiffany and Marsha for the first time.

"Hey!" Kong motioned to his five other crew members. "Da kine wahines* paddle dah canoe foh dah malihinis!"*

Tiffany yelled across the water. "These wahines can beat you kamaainas* anytime!"

For a second, Josh was concerned that his sister's unexpected challenge would anger Kong. Instead, he shrugged. "Maybe so, wit' dah canoe half-full a' watah!"

Marsha snapped, "No more than our canoe. Seems to me we're about even."

Shawn said, "Kong, you know we can beat you easily. But that wouldn't be any fun. What if we bail out our canoes and start the race again?"

Josh couldn't believe what he heard. He stared in surprise at Shawn as Kong laughed and called back. "You still one pupule* malihini! Okay, Bruddah. Bail, den Kong beat you good!"

Shawn turned to his crew. "Everybody bail. It'll drive Kong crazy to have you girls paddling against him. We can beat him. I know we can!"

"Sure, we can!" Tiffany cried. She swung her short, soggy hair out of her eyes, cupped her hands together and began bailing. "Let's do it!"

"Do it!" Marsha echoed, throwing a bucketful of water back into the ocean.

Josh had mixed feelings about Shawn's latest challenge as everyone bailed water out of the canoes. He glanced around for his father's powerboat, but it was still nowhere in sight. Josh was uneasy. Had the Boston Whaler's motor failed? Or was the powerboat just hidden behind the retreating screen of water? Josh tried to think his father would re-appear. The boy went on bailing.

When the canoes were ready, all twelve paddlers took

their seats. Shawn took his place in Seat One. "Ready?" he asked.

Manuel nodded and gave the command. "Reach out!"

Josh had barely gripped his paddle when he heard Kong's Seat Two paddler echo the command. From both canoes, "Hoe!"* sounded as one. All twelve paddlers hit the water almost together and the race was on again!

Josh felt a rush of pure pleasure. The tiredness in his aching muscles fell away. The warm sunshine soothed his back, but the salt water drying on his skin gave him a sticky feeling.

The weather was clear almost to the horizon. The seas were calming fast. The canoes fairly shot through the water.

Josh heard a motor and turned to see his father's boat roaring toward them. Tank waved and Mr. Ladd throttled down to call, "We're mighty glad to see all of you. We lost sight of you in the heavy seas and rain. Then our motor died and was hard to start. Everyone okay?"

"We're doing great!" Tiffany yelled. "We're going to beat Kong, too!"

Her father smiled and waved. "I'll follow you in."

The two outriggers stayed about even across the last of the open sea. This cheered Shawn's crew heartily. They paddled hard. So did Kong's crew. Neither gained on the other as they passed McGregor Point Lighthouse.

Sprint time, Josh thought. *It's now or never!*

The quieter water of Maalaea Bay* made it easier to

paddle. Both canoes shot forward, heading for the small boat harbor.

Josh breathed hard from the extra exertion, but his body seemed to have new strength. He guessed the same was true of his teammates, for they were paddling with quiet joy. Kong's canoe would not pull away from them this time.

In a few minutes, however, Josh glanced again at Kong's canoe and a low moan escaped his lips. "Oh, no! He's starting to pull ahead of us."

Shawn saw what was happening, and called over his shoulders, "Give a little extra!"

Josh tried to summon up some hidden reserve of strength. Still, Kong's outrigger slowly pulled ahead. They had been through so much and had come so close! But now, in the final few hundred yards, they were losing in spite of their best efforts.

"Look!" Tiffany exclaimed. "On shore! There's Mom, Grandma and Nathan!"

"My family, too!" Marsha added. "And there's the Okamotos! See, Roger? There's your family! And Manuel's! Everybody's there, cheering for us!"

Josh added, "And Big K and Little K's parents are here, too."

Everybody except Shawn's parents, Josh thought miserably. *They're never there for him.*

"Hey, everybody!" Shawn cried, "Look! That's my dad and Mom getting out of their car. They made it!"

Josh yelled, "Come on, everybody! Let's make them proud of Shawn!"

"Yea!" Tiffany cried. "Let's win this one for Shawn!"

The canoe racers shouted agreement as Roger called, "Power ten!"

Josh didn't know it was possible to try any harder, but now he not only wanted to beat Kong, but he also wanted Shawn to win for his parents. The sight of everyone on shore, cheering them toward victory, gave Josh new determination.

He paddled so hard and fast he thought he would burst from the exertion, yet he felt a soaring sense of hope.

We're gaining on Kong, Josh thought. *About fifty yards to go! But we've got to catch him and then pass him.*

Slowly, ever so slowly, Shawn's canoe drew even with Kong's. From shore, Josh heard the roaring cheers of family and friends. In spite of their best efforts, Shawn's crew could not pass Kong's canoe.

Twenty-five yards to go! The bows of both canoes seemed tied together evenly. Fifteen! Ten!

"Now!" Roger called. "One more great effort, everyone. Give it all you've got!"

In moments, Josh realized the final desperate paddling was paying off. With agonizing slowness, Shawn's outrigger eased forward.

We're starting to pass them, Josh thought, almost numb from excitement and exhaustion. *Five yards...three... We're pulling ahead! We're going to do it!*

Shawn's canoe flashed across the finish line about five feet ahead of Kong's!

Everyone in Shawn's canoe and on shore broke into wild shouts of joy. "We won! We won!"

Josh couldn't remember a noiser celebration than the one that followed. Even though his throat was sore from yelling, he had never been happier.

When everyone had finished hugging and slapping each other on the back, Josh walked over to his sister and Marsha.

"I'm proud of you, Tif!" he said softly. "You did great! You, too, Marsha!"

"You guys would never have won without us!" his sister yelled happily.

Josh nodded, then looked at Kong. He was staring moodily at his canoe. Josh felt a little awkward, but he walked over to Kong. "No hard feelings, huh?"

Kong started to scowl, then shrugged. "You malihinis lucky!"

Then Josh walked over and thanked Big K and Little K for giving up their seats so the girls could race. After Josh said good-bye to the brothers, he saw Shawn with his parents. Josh couldn't see their faces because they were hugging each other tightly. Josh hoped Shawn's parents realized that he had inspired the crew to do the seemingly impossible, in spite of many difficulties.

A lot of things are going to change, Josh thought happily. *I won't have to worry about Rick's bothering me.*

I can hardly wait for the police to explain what that was all about.

In the Ladd family's apartment that night, Sergeant Tomashima explained what had happened. "Some time ago, Rick and Larry robbed a Honolulu wholesale diamond salesman of about a quarter-million dollars in unset stones. After that, Rick and Larry had a disagreement, so Rick decided to cut his partner out and sell the diamonds by himself. That's how you got involved, Josh."

"Oh? How so?"

"Rick made arrangements to meet a fence* who works out of a boat. They agreed to meet off Molokini.* Larry learned about the plan and followed Rick. When Rick saw Larry bearing down on him, Rick panicked. He had to get rid of the diamonds before Larry caught him, so Rick gave them to you and then swam off. Larry didn't see that happen. He continued to follow Rick, but he escaped.

"But there are no secrets in the underworld," said Sergeant Tomashima. "Somebody told Larry that Rick was meeting you at Diamond Head,* so Larry showed up in the tunnel. But none of you knew that I was also there."

Josh exclaimed, "You're the one who tripped Larry so I could escape!"

The detective nodded. "Later, I caught Larry and recovered the gems he had burglarized from your apartment. But we still couldn't find Rick, so our department had to play a waiting game. Rick thought you had the diamonds, and we knew he would keep trying to recover them. But we didn't dare tell you or your family what was going on, or you might have accidentally tipped Rick off."

"How did you know Rick was coming after me at the canoe race?"

"We have our sources," the detective said evasively. "We found out this morning that Rick was going to follow you during the race to try to recover the jewels. As you know, we used the helicopter to pick him up. The police department is grateful for the help you and your family and friends gave us in closing the case."

After the officer had gone, Josh's family discussed the exciting events of the last several days.

"I'm glad Shawn's parents came," Josh said. "It's what helped us win the race."

Tiffany agreed. "Yes, and Shawn seemed different this afternoon, as if he's not only proved something to himself, but to his parents, also."

Grandma Ladd stopped her knitting and said softly, "Joshua, I'm so pleased that you and your friends didn't gloat over Kong's defeat. He should treat you nicely and respect all of you from now on."

Josh shook his head. "I hope so, but I doubt it."

Josh's mother sighed. "I'm just glad it's all over! When I think how close all of you came to being hurt...."

Her husband reached out and put his arm around her shoulder comfortingly.

Grandma said, "You children all did a very wonderful

thing in helping those men in the swamped canoe. Doing what's right is more important than anything else. As the Scripture says, 'Do not withhold good from those to whom it is due, when it is in your power to do it.' "*

Josh's father added, "I think you also learned that satisfaction was not in beating Kong but in seeing how Shawn came out of it."

Josh mused, "Yeah! And maybe his parents will realize how important having time with him really is, and they'll be there for him more often."

Josh paused, then added, "I keep thinking of Kong. He was so sure he could beat us that he had developed a wrong attitude. But that also made me realize I was wrong in wanting to get even with Kong. Look at the trouble it got me into—and my friends, too."

That night as Josh said his prayers, he whispered, "I'm sorry about wanting to get even. Help me, so I won't do that again."

He lay awake for a long time, thinking of the great Hawaiian canoe race. Then his mind drifted to other possible adventures. *I'd like to be in a surfing championship someday.* He was still thinking of the wonderful adventures he could have when he drifted off to sleep.

GLOSSARY

Chapter One

Aloha shirt: (*ah-low-hah* shirt) A loose-fitting man's Hawaiian shirt worn outside the pants. The garment is usually very colorful.

Bruddah: (*brud-duh*) Pidgin English for "brother."

Cat': An abbreviation for catamaran, which is a boat.

Catamaran: (*cat-ah-ma-ran*) A boat with twin hulls, side by side.

Da kine: (*dah-kine*) Pidgin English for "the kind." This is more of an expression and is therefore not usually translated literally.

Islet: (*eye-let*) A little island.

Lanyard: (*lan-yard*) A pull string on an air canister that is attached to a life jacket. If a diver gets in trouble underwater and needs to come to the surface, he or she pulls the lanyard and the canister pumps air into the life jacket.

Maalaea Bay: (*ma-ah-lay-ah* bay) An ocean bay on

the island of Maui, which is a port for pleasure and fishing boats.

Malihini: (*mah-lee-hee-nee*) Hawaiian for "newcomer."

Molokini: (*ma-low-kee-nee*) An islet that's really the tip of an ancient volcano rising from the ocean floor. The U.S. Coast Guard maintains an unmanned beacon light on this uninhabited speck of land.

Muumuu: (*moo-oo-moo-oo*) A loose, colorful dress or gown frequently worn by women in Hawaii. This word is sometimes mispronounced as "moo-moo."

Planty: (*plant-ee*) Pidgin English for "plenty."

Pontoon: The float of an outrigger canoe.

Pupule: (*poo-poo-lay*) Hawaiian for "crazy."

Simon Legree: (*s-eye-men le-gree*) The brutal slave owner in the novel *Uncle Tom's Cabin*.

Trough: (*trof*) A long and narrow depression between high waves that looks like a tube.

Chapter Two

Ala Wai Canal: (*ah-lah why* canal) Ala Wai Canal is a man-made waterway on the island of Oahu.

Aloha shirt: (*ah-low-hah* shirt) A colorful Hawaiian shirt.

Be-still tree: A short tree with dense green foliage and bright yellow flowers that fold up at night.

Bow: (*bough*) The forward part of the canoe.

Bruddah: (*brud-duh*) Brother.

Catamaran: (*kat-a-ma-ran*) A boat with twin hulls.

Da kine: (*dah-kine*) The kind.

Diamond Head: A prominent volcanic landmark.

Haole: (*how-lee*) A Hawaiian word originally meaning "stranger" but now used to mean Caucasians, or white people.

Koa: (*ko-ah*) Lumber from the koa tree was originally used for making outrigger canoes.

Lanai: (*lay-nay-ee*) A patio, porch, or balcony. Also, when capitalized, a smaller Hawaiian island.

Maalaea Bay: (*ma-ah-lay-ah* bay) An ocean bay on the island of Maui.

Mahalo: (*maw-hah-low*) Thanks.

Malihini: (*mah-lee-hee-nee*) Newcomer.

Molokini: (*ma-low-kee-nee*) An islet that's really the tip of an ancient volcano rising from the ocean floor.

Mynah bird: (*mi-nah* bird) A black Asian bird of the starling family. In Hawaii, some of these birds are kept as pets and taught to mimic speech.

Pilikia: (*pee-lee-kee-ah*) Hawaiian for "trouble."

Pupule: (*poo-poo-lay*) Crazy.

Waikiki Beach: (*why-kee-kee* beach) This beach, on the island of Oahu, is a popular tourist attraction.

Zoris: (*zor-eez*) Flat, thonged sandals usually made of straw, leather, or rubber.

Chapter Three

Akamai: (*ah-kah-my*) Hawaiian for "smart, intelligent."

Ala Wai Canal: (*ah-lah why* canal) A man-made waterway.

Banana tree: (*buh-nan-uh*) Bananas in Hawaii grow in small shrubs or trees with long, wide leaves. These bananas are used mostly for cooking.

Board and batten house: A house with a particular style of siding. Wide boards or sheets of lumber are set vertically, and the joints are covered by small strips of wood (battens).

Kanaka: (*kah-nah-kah*) Hawaiian man.

Kewalo Basin: (*kee-wa-low* basin) This ocean basin is the home port for charter and sight-seeing boats.

Molokini: (*ma-low-kee-nee*) An islet that's really the tip of an ancient volcano rising from the ocean floor.

Muumuu: (*moo-oo-moo-oo*) A colorful dress or gown.

Mynah bird: (*mi-nah* bird) A black Asian bird.

Pau: (*pow*) The Hawaiian word for "finished" or "all done."

Plumeria: (*ploo-mar-y-ah*) A shrub or small tree that produces large, fragrant blossoms.

Waikiki: (*why-kee-kee*) A popular beach on the island of Oahu.

Zoris: (*zor-eez*) Flat, thonged sandals.

Chapter Four

Ala Wai Canal: (*ah-lah why* canal) A man-made waterway.

Be-still tree: A short tree with bright yellow flowers.

Bruddah: (*brud-duh*) Brother.

Da kine: (*dah-kine*) The kind.

Gunwales: The upper edge of the canoe's side.

Haole: (*how-lee*) Caucasian; white.

Hoe: (*ho-ay*) To paddle or a paddle for a canoe.

Huhu: (*hoo-hoo*) Hawaiian for "angry."

Koolau Range: (*koh-oh-low* range) The volcanic mountains that rise directly behind Honolulu.

Molokini: (*ma-low-kee-nee*) An islet that's really the tip of an ancient volcano rising from the ocean floor.

Oleanders: (*oh-lee-an-derz*) Poisonous evergreen shrubs with fragrant flowers in white, pink, or red.

Pilikia: (*pee-lee-kee-ah*) Trouble.

Planty: (*plant-ee*) Plenty.

Waikiki: (*why-kee-kee*) A popular beach on the island of Oahu.

Chapter Five

Ala Wai Canal: (*ah-lah why* canal) A man-made waterway.

Aloha shirt: (*ah-low-hah* shirt) A colorful Hawaiian shirt.

Diamond Head: A prominent volcanic landmark.

Monkeypod tree: An ornamental tropical tree that

has clusters of flowers, sweet pods eaten by cattle, and wood used in carving.

Puka: (*poo-kah*) A hole or a doorway.

Chapter Seven

Ala Wai Canal: (*ah-lah why* canal) A man-made waterway.

Aloha shirt: (*ah-low-hah* shirt) A colorful Hawaiian shirt.

Aloha: (*ah-low-hah*) A popular Hawaiian word with varied meanings, including hello, goodbye, and love.

Aloha nui: (*ah-low-hah noo-ee*) Much love.

Bougainvillea: (*boge-in-vee-ah*) A tropical woody vine with brilliant purple or red clusters of flowers.

E Ko Makou Makua Iloko O Ka Lani: (*e ko mah-ko-u ma-ku-ah ee-low-ko oh ka lah-nee*) The beginning of the Lord's Prayer: "Our Father who art (is) in heaven...." (Matthew 6:9, RSV)

Hapa haole: (*hah-pah how-lee*) Half or part white.

Hibiscus: (*hi-bis-cus*) Hawaii's state flower. It has a large, open blossom and is available in many colors. No particular color, however, is designated for the state flower.

Ke Mele Hoomaikai: (*ke me-le hoo-ma-eye-ka-eye*) A song of praise.

Kala: (*kah-lah*) Hawaiian for Carl.

Kamaaina: (*kham-ah-eye-nah*) A Hawaiian word meaning "child of the land," or "native."

Kanaka: (*kah-nah-kah*) Hawaiian man.

Koma: (*ko-mah*) Hawaiian for Tom.

Leis: (*lay-eez*) Flower necklaces that are given to people on arrival to Hawaii and sometimes on departure.

Muumuu: (*moo-oo-moo-oo*) A colorful dress or gown.

Chapter Eight

Da kine: (*dah-kine*) The kind.

Damocles: (*dam-a-klez*) A fictional character in an ancient story who was sitting at a big dinner, and a sword was hanging over his head suspended by a single hair.

Haole: (*how-lee*) Caucasian; white.

Hoe: (*ho-ay*) To paddle or a paddle for a canoe.

Kamaaina: (*kham-ah-eye-nah*) Child of the land; native.

Lanai: (*lay-nay-ee*) A patio, porch, or balcony.

Molokini: (*ma-low-kee-nee*) An islet that's really the tip of an ancient volcano rising from the ocean floor.

Pupule: (*poo-poo-lay*) Crazy.

Chapter Nine

Ala Wai Canal: (*ah-lah why* canal) A man-made waterway.

Damocles: (*dam-a-klez*) A man at a banquet with a sword hanging over him.

Haole: (*how-lee*) Caucasian; white.

Hoe: (*ho-ay*) To paddle or a paddle for a canoe.

Lanai: (*lay-nay-ee*) A patio, porch, or balcony.

Chapter Ten

Ala Wai Canal: (*ah-lah why* canal) A man-made waterway.

Be-still tree: A short tree with bright yellow flowers.

Da kine: (*dah-kine*) The kind.

Haole: (*how-lee*) Caucasian; white.

Hoe: (*ho-ay*) To paddle or a paddle for a canoe.

Huhu: (*hoo-hoo*) Angry.

Planty: (*plant-ee*) Plenty.

Chapter Eleven

Buddhist (*bood-hust*) A person who follows the religion that grew out of the teaching of Gautama Buddha.

Cumulonimbus clouds: (*kue-mah-low-nim-bus*) Clouds, reaching great heights, which look like huge mounds of whipped cream.

Da kine: (*dah-kine*) The kind.

Haole: (*how-lee*) Caucasian; white.

Hoe: (*ho-ay*) To paddle or a paddle for a canoe.

Huhu: (*hoo-hoo*) Angry.

Kona: (*ko-nah*) A south wind.

Lanai: (*lay-nay-ee*) A patio, porch, or balcony.

Maalaea Bay: (*ma-ah-lay-ah* bay) An ocean bay on the island of Maui.

Malihini: (*mah-lee-hee-nee*) Newcomer.

Molokini: (*ma-low-kee-nee*) An islet that's really the tip of an ancient volcano rising from the ocean floor.

Planty: (*plant-ee*) Plenty.

Wikiwiki: (*wee-kee-wee-kee*) Hawaiian for "hurry."

Chapter Twelve

Hoe: (*ho-ay*) To paddle or a paddle for a canoe.

Maalaea Bay: (*ma-ah-lay-ah* bay) An ocean bay on the island of Maui.

Molokini: (*ma-low-kee-nee*) An islet that's really the tip of an ancient volcano rising from the ocean floor.

Chapter Thirteen

Cumulonimbus cloud: (*kue-mah-low-nim-bus*) Clouds that reach great heights.

Maalaea Bay: (*ma-ah-lay-ah* bay) An ocean bay on the island of Maui.

Molokini: (*ma-low-kee-nee*) An islet that's really the tip of an ancient volcano rising from the ocean floor.

Chapter Fourteen

Bruddah: (*brud-duh*) Brother.

Da kine: (*dah-kine*) The kind.

Diamond Head: A prominent volcanic landmark.

Fence: Someone who receives stolen goods from the person who took them.

Hoe: (*ho-ay*) To paddle or a paddle for a canoe.

Kamaaina: (*kham-ah-eye-nah*) Child of the land; native.

Maalaea Bay: (*ma-ah-lay-ah* bay) An ocean bay on the island of Maui.

Malihini: (*mah-lee-hee-nee*) Newcomer.

Molokini: (*ma-low-kee-nee*) An islet that's really the tip of an ancient volcano rising from the ocean floor.

Proverbs 3:27, RSV: The verse Josh's grandmother quotes.

Pupule: (*poo-poo-lay*) Crazy.

Wahine: (*wah-hee-nay*) Hawaiian for "female."